MW01616783

BUDDY GREEN

James W. Haley, Jr.

LAMBETH HOUSE LIBRARY

Copyright © 2022 James W. Haley, Jr.

All rights reserved.

ISBN: 978-0-578-31499-0

This work is dedicated to the memory of Odessa Lee Green, born at Cherry Hill farm, Culpeper County, Virginia, on January 16, 1890.

The City (1910)

"... Don't hope for elsewhere—
There is no ship for you, there is no road.
As you have wasted your life here,
In this small corner, so you have ruined it on the
whole earth"

C.P. Cavafy

1

Lead has been mined in Germanic lands for three thousand years. Substantial deposits were located in Saxony at Beinsdorf, in Westphalia at Lanerthal, and in Siegel in the Hartz Mountains. But the lead with which we will be following came from a small town near Llimenau, located on the Thuringian Wald, nine hundred and fifty miles above the level of the sea. Llimenau is thirty miles southwest of Weimar and forty miles southeast of Eisenach, where Bach was born. If you choose to make the calculations, a triangulation of these three towns reveals a geometry Pythagorean and orderly, mathematical and taxisian.

Lead was recovered as a product of the smelting of galena, a combination of lead and sulphur, some with a content of silver. It was processed primarily for the small quantities of silver. The smelting consisted of roasting the galena and reduction techniques developed in the ancient near East, and spread westwards in Mycenaean times from Asia Minor to Crete, to the Aegean, to the Greek mainland, to Rome, and to Germanic lands. Lead weighs four times the weight of silver, and thus sinks to the bottom of the melt during the smelting process—the silver to be skimmed off. The sulfur burns away. The lead remains.

....

By the turn of the twentieth century, Cherry Hill was the

residue of a much larger farm, one that had been in the Green family since 1728, its continued ownership drifting among family members over the years, until devolving upon Buddy's father, James Edwin Green, when he attained the age of twenty-one.

It was located in the northwest corner of Culpeper County, adjacent to the west was Rappahannock County. About 4 miles from the farm was a hamlet named Amissville, while the town of Culpeper was 19 miles to the southeast. Most county roads were, at best, graveled. Local state roads were inconsistently paved.

Amissville was little more than a country store / satellite post office. It was located on the well paved state road, Route 218, between Warrenton and Sperryville. There were available staples—sugar, salt, pepper, kerosene, matches, canned lard, aspirin, bandages, iodine, hard candy, bags of tobacco, rolling papers, packs of manufactured cigarettes from Richmond, cheap cigars, pints of Lydia Pinkham's, an herbal tonic for indisposed or overly nervous ladies—and local honey, dried fruit, cured smoked hams, and fresh farm vegetables and fruits.The store was named Hubert's. Sometimes, if you knew treasured and coveted passwords, moonshine could appear.

But it was never run by a man named Hubert, in anyone's memory. It was first run by Hugh Davis, then by Bobby Hamm. Neither were from Culpeper County, it was thought. Both were deemed honest, though one was unseemly critical, and the other usually falling half-asleep.

On land next door to the store were also two primitive steel silos, one for excess farm wheat and one for excess farm corn, owned by a corporation in Warrenton. The contributions by farmers were carefully measured and recorded in bushels by the owner's name, and thus calibrated for respective payment when the contents were purchased, as each grain from all farmers was intermixed in the appropriate silo. There was no rental for space in the silos, because the corporation set the price, without competition, for the grains when purchased. Most farmers thought the prices were relatively fair, relying on reports of distant prices, occasionally received.

Of greatest significance in Amissville was Amissville Methodist Church. It was quite well attended. It was almost as large as the Methodist church in the town of Culpeper. It had been sturdily built, and added upon in the passing years, atop a slight rise. It had its own well, a large fireplace, a foot-powered organ, prayer books and hymnals for all, an open covered shed for picnics and leaders' meetings, robes for a choir.

But what made it so attractive a venue for excellent ministers was the fact there was an adjacent glebe, a home that could comfortably house a family of four, with a private well and outdoor facility, and furnished with somewhat fine furnishings. Thus, ministers demonstrated care, love, generosity, eloquence, for their flock, mindful that their tenure depended upon the continuing approval by the older, male, well-to-do, devoted members. It was an unsaid survival challenge for the finest men of the cloth. But most enjoyed a long tenure. And the most excellent attracted believers far from Amissville. These added appreciable amounts to the collection plate, a fact not unnoticed.

Hubert's always remained open on Sundays, from 8 a.m. to 3 p.m. to accommodate the many who attended Amissville Methodist.

....

The acreage of Cherry Hill had been much reduced during the years 1866 to 1870. Yankee carpetbaggers, or their despised local minions, had been installed by the U.S. Government, as the government of Culpeper County. They purposely imposed punitive property taxes on the larger farms to break them up, knowing their owners could not pay, and divided up those acres forfeited for redistribution. These individuals purchased many such parcels, at tax auction, for their profitable resale. And they were always properly re-surveyed, at taxpayer expense.

So Cherry Hill was now composed of 77 ¾ acres. It was bordered on the east by Indian Run, and its other dimensions by property of others, some whose names were unknown.

Entrance was a lane, connecting to the north to a county road.

There were open fields, though much fewer than in the past, and scattered small woodlots, their stands of trees remaining untimbered, as insurance for the necessary firewood in an unsure future. They purchased wood for their needs.

The farmhouse was two storied, with a tin roof, and two fireplaces, other than the small one serving the iron kitchen stove. From the upper porch one could see the distant Blue Ridge Mountains, thrice pierced by roads heading east and west, otherwise the barrier to the Shenandoah Valley.

The farmhouse and the barn stood on ground naturally level, but cresting the top hill, reduced by wind and rain over centuries. There were three apple trees in the yard, four English walnut, and eleven flowering cherry trees.

Once, a generation ago, a Green had returned from Amissville Methodist on a Palm Sunday, bringing a sprig of Weeping Willow used in the service. The sprig was rooted in a glass of water, and planted in the front yard. Now, a substantial tree of that species adorned the location.

Wild cherry trees were abundant among the oaks in the woodlots. On this hill also were the kitchen garden, outdoor facilities, small outbuildings, a chicken coop, with the surrounding acreage sloping slightly downward. At the bottom of this truncated hill, at its steepest, was a spring, the only other source of freshwater, Indian Run too distant.

One former field, not used within anyone's present memory, terminating at Indian Run, was now scattered with large oaks, both red and white, with open fallow ground between them. What was fascinating, though, were the piles of rocks, interspersed within the old field, stacked in old corners in ages past, to clear a rocky field for planting.

The present open fields were used to grow, in the main, corn and, to a lesser extent, wheat. These crops could provide some cash.

Into this world was born Buddy Green.

....

James Lewis Green was born on September 28, 1898, in the house at Cherry Hill farm, in Culpeper County, Virginia. His father was James Edwin Green. His mother was Janie Wood Green. He had three older sisters, and three older half-siblings, two boys and a girl. He was christened on October 7, 1898, at Amissville Methodist Church. That year the United States was at war—with Spain.

....

The origin of lead is Uranium 238. It is created—by time and physics — when Uranium 238 decays in progressive degrees— into thorium, radium, polonium—each orderly progression spinning off protons and electrons, until the formation of lead stabilizes the mutation. There the destruction by time and physics end. Nature has created lead.

An atom of lead has 82 electrons spinning about in orbits and balancing the 82 protons within its nucleus. But all atoms of lead are not the same. There are isotopes of lead. An isotope is a tiny aberration of atoms in an element. The isotope of lead, called lead 88, has 88 electrons and 88 protons, slightly greater in mass, but still in balance, or valence. The creation of this isotope is random, unordered, but once created, it is orderly in structure.

The isotope is contained in a much larger piece of the classically balanced lead. Lead containing this isotope was mined near Llimenau.

Because of this isotope we can trace, or track the lead. We shall do so. Hereafter, this is our lead.

2

June 10, 1900

The child became sick, very sick, quickly as a spring rainstorm. His mother thought snake bite—copperhead. She knew no antidote. But they had searched the screened-in porch, where the child lies in his crib on a folded blanket, and found no snake. Examined, his body shows no puncture marks.

The child is gagging, spitting, rolling, his arms waving in the air, his legs kicking, his face red. Sister Janie ran to her bed. Odessa was praying just inside the open door to the parlor. Eliza stood by, watching. All were crying.

His mother was rocking back and forth on each leg, picking up the baby and then replacing him in the crib. Her eyes were widened in terror.

Eliza looked out into the road next to the house. There Clatterbuck's negro overseer had finished unloading yard-tall cylinders of white oak for splitting, from a two horse wagon. She called for him, screaming, "Help, help, please!"

Thus summoned, he slowly approached the porch, and climbed the two stairs leading upward. He wore a worn, tattered, blue, cotton shirt with attached pants, held up by shoulder straps. His chest was bare.

On that chest hung a poultice on a strand of violaceous yarn. They saw it as hideous.

Rumor had it as a man's privates, dried and raveling, or perhaps a mutilated root, unknown to us, pulled from the earth in secret by such men, perhaps a legacy from Africa.

The poltice purls as he bends over the child. His finger touches the child on his face, neck, between his toes. He straightens up and looks at Jane Wood Green and Eliza. "The poltice will not work," he says. His eyes appear phosphorescent in the twilight.

From his pocket he brings a candle, bees-wax. He lights it and holds it before the child's mouth—drawing it backwards and forward, keeping the flame and corona upright—in rhythm with the child's gasps.

Towards that light, which later the mother and Eliza feel is evidence of God's golden splendor, flutteringly flies a hornet, first perching on the child's lip, its venom left in the child's swollen throat; then it struggles toward the coruscated flame, touches it, and falls a burned and lopsided vespine imago to the pine-planked floor. The candle extinguished itself, a trace of tarry smoke vanishing in the summer air. The man replaced the candle in his pocket.

The calico cat crushed and chewed the remnant of the hornet.

So instructed, Eliza brought cold water in the child's tin cup, and, raising him upright, gave him repeated sips. The child is now calm, red retreating from his face, evenly breathing, approaching sleep. A thaumaturgic moment.

His mother gave this blessed man two hoarded silver dollars, which he placed in a shirt pocket. After nodding, and without a word, he left the porch and seated himself on the empty wagon, languidly pulled up the lane, to the County road.

They never saw him again. Later they learned his given name was July and that he had left Clatterbuck's, having purchased a farm for himself in adjacent Rappahannock County.

....

Eliza began to refer to James, as her "little buddy," as

eventually did her sisters. They treated him as their own child, their baby. His first spoken word was "buddy." And by that name he was thereafter known, from the time he was two years old. "James" dissolved in the past, almost as a fleeting mist.

....

The first and third Mondays in January, April, July, and October were Rules Day for the Circuit Court of Culpeper County. The Circuit Court judge traveled within his circuit to the various courthouses: Culpeper, in Culpeper County; the town of Washington, or "Little Washington," as it was called, in Rappahannock County; Warrenton, in Fauquier County; Orange, in Orange County. The counties were contiguous. Each had its separate Rules Days.

On Rules Days, parties could present orders for entry by the court, file pleadings beginning new cases or pleadings in cases already on the docket, make various motions, and set cases for trial. A Rules Day, moreover, marked the beginning, the first day, of the term—usually the following four days—during which the Circuit Court would hear and determine cases.

The Circuit Court judge was only concerned with important cases: felonies where someone could go to prison for more than a year, disputes involving land, claims for more than $100. Minor matters were handled by the justice of the peace, old Barton Fry, who wasn't even a lawyer, on the two days a week when he stumbled into the courthouse, some said drunk, from his regular job as a cabinetmaker.

Rules Days had evolved into market days. People had to serve as jurors, as witnesses, as plaintiffs or defendants; and in their wake came their spouses, their children, their neighbors and, for those who could afford it, their lawyers. But more, those second Mondays was a time for one to bring to Culpeper your produce, your butter, your eggs, your horses, your cattle, sheep, mules, dogs, chickens, Guineas for sale or barter. And what better time for the myriad local merchants—of clothes, tools, buggies, guns, ammunition, salt, pins, sugar, coffee, candy, saddles, bridles, tobacco, medicines, nails—to open

early and stay late; to have your broken tools mended by
Tublecain, the blacksmith; for the itinerant peddlers to trundle
into town behind their horse-drawn wagons; for purveyors of
whiskey to arrive from the mountains; for the gamblers and
loose women to gather in certain rooms in the Lord Fairfax
Hotel. And what better time to sell grander whiskey, much
better whiskey, one with a label—Bumgardner Rye or the
finaries from up north that got to the Shenandoah Valley
through the railroad down there from rich manufacturing
Yankee land, to Winchester or Staunton, thence over the
mountain gap to Culpeper. One could buy a hat or mirror or
dress from Pittsburgh if you had the money. Rules Day became
a holiday from hard work.

It was a family fair, a carnival, a country revelry. There were
games for children; theatrical and music performances;
recitations from Shakespeare; sermons by deranged self-
anointed preachers; tales of the War from Confederate
veterans; boxing matches and horse races; games of chance or
of skill; an occasional Gypsy fortune teller; sellers of tonics to
cure any problems of health, body, or mind; and a black man,
Jules, the One-Man-Band (who claimed to be 95 years old and
a former slave from South Carolina). His band consisted of
him on a guitar (not a banjo), a whistle, and a single drum,
which his foot powered with a lever. He played what he called
"the blues." His whistle offered many tones. Buddy would
remember one of them, years later at Camp Lee, Virginia. But
the greatest entertainment of all was the proceedings in the
Circuit Court. Always open to the public.

There were heard the pleas for mercy, the spectrum of truth
to falsehood in the testimony of the parties and their
witnesses, the wondrous excuses and fantastic claims, the
perorations of the lawyers—like the Sophists despised by Plato
—trying to make the lesser appear the better cause, spouting
of Coke and Blackstone, of this and that section of the Code of
Virginia, and of old cases decided by the Supreme Court of
Appeals of Virginia. Those lawyers, in whispers, with shouts,
with feigned tears of righteous anger, whirling and pointing

like dervishes, waving old books, all seeking only justice or, rather, what they deemed just for their client. Lawyers in their prime with justified reputations for oratory or knowledge or, exceptionally, even both. Those lawyers young, their economic and political futures determined by their present performances, measured by the judge, by other lawyers, by parties and witnesses and spectators. Those lawyers old, beholden to alcohol or of failing mind or memory, stumbling in their arguments, not current on the law, to be avoided by those not desperate or destitute.

Over this spectacle presided Circuit Court Judge Lee Wood Russell, with a firm hand and the respect of the lawyers. There was no foolishness, except for the lawyers, of course; there was humor; there was displayed a vast knowledge of the law; there was mercy; there was understanding; but, most of all, there was in all men's view justice in Judge Russell's court. He had come to Culpeper on this Rules Day, Monday, April 6, 1911, to preside

. . . .

Judge Russell was from Cedar Mountain, located east of Culpeper in the county. His father, Washington Russell, had owned a fine farm called Ashton, a prosperous store, and a gristmill, on Robinson Creek, which flowed in a narrow valley at the base of the mountain, and thence to larger Rapidan River. In July 1863, a Yankee cavalry unit from Michigan burned both the store and the gristmill for no apparent reason other than, perhaps, they had stolen all the contents of each and saw no reason to leave them standing. Two days later, on July 14, Washington Russell was killed by the Michigan soldiers, it was said, after he purposely gut-shot their Captain with a .44 caliber Navy Colt pistol, that Captain returning to water his horse near the destroyed mill. Judge Russell never spoke of the circumstances of his father's death.

This tale from the War was legend. As was Judge Russell's poverty as a child, his brilliance at the law school in Charlottesville, his reputation as the lawyer to retain, his fairness, his appointment as Circuit Court judge when he was only 37. There were also other parts to the legend of the Russells, about which men only hinted, and then only quietly. It was said that Washington Russell and the other mill owners in Culpeper County, including Marcus Thompson, a free black, would meet once a month in the even-then called Lord Fairfax Hotel to discuss the cost of milling a bushel of grain. And to take of Thompson's whiskey, reported too be the finest in Culpeper, better than any that could be store-bought or brought over from the mountains in the west. The whiskey, it was said, was aged in three oak barrels that Thompson had obtained from his uncle, also a free black.

The cost of milling was set, always a little less for the Negroes who milled at Thompson's, but not so much less to attract notice by the white farmers. And besides making the finest whiskey, Thompson was reported to be the best businessman of the lot, highly respected for that acumen and his integrity, and quite rich—quietly so, of course. He lent money to white businessmen, as a reasonable rate, and his fellow mill owners made sure, quite sure, that Thompson was repaid, in full, with interest, and on time. A failed businessman named Rose who had cheated and slandered Thompson disappeared, his whereabouts never discovered. His debt to Thompson, though, it was heard, was jointly honored by the mill owners.

In short, Thompson was a respected friend of these gentlemen, though that friend always entered the Lord Fairfax from the rear, at night, and no one ever acknowledged that such meetings ever took place. And Thompson had a beautiful sister, Mary, who Russell was said, in a whisper, to have admired.

One month after the destruction of Russell's mill, Thompson burnt down his own. The Yankee soldiers wanted the grain they had stolen from the local farmers milled for free for them, because of "what they had done for the other slaves." Thompson refused, told them he was not, and never had been, a slave. So the Yankees threw Thompson off his property and began to run the mill themselves. Six nights later, the mill burned and Thompson shot himself in a stream known as Indian Run. He was found by a boy picking blackberries.

No one ever found Thompson's money, though the Yankees looked hard, having heard the rumors of his wealth. They had men out digging up the ground where the mill had stood. Thompson had no surviving family, other than his sister Mary and her son Solon Thompson, whose fairness of skin dictated the race of his father, but that father remained unknown, or unnamed.

These survivors were taken in by Ann Wood Russell, Washington Russell's widow, at what remained of her husband's farm. And so it was also said, that Lee and Solon were raised together, "almost like brothers." Lee was older, by two years.

It was Solon Thompson who lived with Judge Russell, and drove Russell's two-horse carriage as they proceeded around the circuit, and always ate lunch with Russell in the restaurants on that circuit. Once that arrangement had been challenged in a Warrenton establishment, and that challenge was forever disbursed, throughout the circuit, when Judge Russell had then wordlessly withdrawn his father's pistol from the holster on his hip.

And it was Solon Thompson who rang the bell, the one on the courthouse lawn, announcing the beginning of the term, and called the docket, when the Court proceeded through the circuit. And protected the Judge if any violence might flare.

....

Judge Russell, on April 6, 1911:
You are Mrs. Green, are you not, ma'am?
Yes, Jane Wood Green.
Your sister was Anne Wood Green?
Yes, she died from the consumption, leaving 3 children.
And you married her widower, James Green?
Yes, sir, their children were my nieces and nephews, and we thought they needed a family.
You have children with Mr. Green?
Yes, four. Three girls, one boy.

That is a right smart number of family.
Yes, sir, it is.
Do you all still live on the family place, up near Amissville?
Well, some are married and gone off, but my children Eliza, Janie, Odessa, and James are still there, thankfully.
What was the name of that farm? I do not remember.
Cherry Hill, sir.
I understand, respectfully, your husband was hurt by the war, as a boy. I heard you people up there were keeping horses for Colonel Mosby, by a spring in the woods, and your husband got found out and, well, hurt, both in the mind and otherwise. The Yankees caused damage, without need. I do not mean to speak of unpleasant matters; but I have heard, as have many others, of that incident and of your husband's bravery at the time.
Yes, the incident has long troubled him; he was only eleven when they horsewhipped him for keeping those horses. He couldn't do anything to help himself, being so young. He was only eleven, and sometimes, it seems those memories cause him to do things perhaps he should not. But he was my husband and I loved him.
Loved him? Is he still with us?
No sir. He was trampled by a horse gone wild, I am told, at the races held at Mr. Hawkins' farm. Some said he was in the drink. He was a good man but, I fear, not a good Methodist. The Yankees ultimately destroyed him. He died almost four years ago. He is buried at Amissville Methodist. Those Yankees stole his family silver, I think it came from England, and they burnt down all the outbuildings—the barn, the ice house, the smokehouse. They burnt it all down. And they took all the food. He told me they saved some pork, that still did not have skippers in it, some parched corn and some dried cherries. They buried it in a bag, one covered with wax, I think. It kept them alive.
Who were these soldiers?
I do not directly know, sir, but I understand they were horse soldiers from Michigan.
Again, Mrs. Green, I understand Cherry Hill is much reduced—

in acreage, I mean—and with missing silver plate. Do you understand we are related? You and your sister are my first cousins. I know our family is a long time from England, but we are here, are we not?

Well, thank you, sir, for that expression. I always believed all us Woods here were related. And I have heard of you, Judge, as a relation.

On another subject, is that boy one of yours? The one with you?

Yes, sir. He is my youngest and only boy.

How old?

Thirteen. His name is James Lewis Green, but we call him Buddy.

....

On Monday, April 6, 1911, in Culpeper:

After scheduled matters had been concluded, Judge Russell inquired:

Mr. Thompson, what else have we upon our docket today?

There is a railroad claim, Judge, by the Alexandria and Orange.

Yes, I see Mr. Nagotte here. Down from up north, Mr. Nagotte, have you a claim?

I do, indeed, Judge. A man came aboard in Alexandria and paid no fare. We put him off here. We have his baggage, Judge, two trunks, leather bound. They contain only books, and some old clothes and some kind of mechanical instruments. They ought to fetch the cost of fare, when you authorize the sale.

As has been my experience with you, Mr. Nagotte, you play too fast and loose with the law. I do not permit that. By what right did you open this man's luggage outside the presence of the court, and why do you presume I shall authorize any sale?

Well, I'd did not want to waste the court's time.

You may be sure, sir, that you shall not. What is the amount of your claim?

$15 for the fare, plus what I determine are my costs ($38) and, of course, my attorney's fees, which you can award.

Describe your costs.

Well, there was the filing fee of $2 for the attachment

proceeding, and general costs.

Please remember attorney's fees.

You are paid a salary by the railroad, are you not? Why, then, additional attorney's fees? What are your "general costs," sir? Certainly, recovery of the filing fee is authorized by law, but you have shown no others. One shall not be grasping in this court.

Where is the owner?

Present.

Your name, sir?

Dr. Andrew Duncan Wills, m'lord.

We have no lords in Virginia, only judges.

Yes, m'lord.

Be cautious, Dr. Wills.

I beg your pardon. I am only familiar with procedure in Scotland.

These trunks are yours? You own all the items in them? And are all the items accounted for?

Aye, sir.

Are you a physician?

Oh, no, I am a doctor of natural philosophy, a man of the Scottish philosophers. Andrew, from the Greek, means "manly," and Duncan, from the Gaelic, means "princely warrior." I fear I may not deserve either appellation, but then that is not here and now. That was when I lived at Dunnattor, in spirit, I think. Dunnattor, on the east coast of Scotland, the castle. You know it, sir, my ancestral home.

Only from a lithograph; on a bleak promontory, if I remember, and in ruins. Your ancestors must have lived there many years ago.

We have come down a little, over the years, mainly to Edinburgh and then to Glasgow. But, as I advised, the spirit lives on. Are you, too, a man of the Enlightenment? Do you know Greek? Any geology? Certainly, John Locke?

Again, be cautious, doctor. One does not cross examine the court.

Cross examine? Oh, you mean cross question. Of course not. Please forgive me. I inquire too much, of all things.

Why are you here, in Culpeper?

I thought I was going to Richmond, where one might seek a position, as a tutor, perhaps. Or something. My trunks contain my library, the foundation, indeed the glorious fountain, of that knowledge I wish to impart to those who seek to learn. My books, fossils, too. I am a traveling university, I hope. I was perhaps confused as to the proper railroad line, or the cost of travel. Bawsed, truth be told.

"Bawsed"?

Aye. We shall learn some Scots, m'lord. Bawsed means inebriated, too many nips, you understand. It happens. That, I think, is why I am short on the fare.

You cannot pay?

I fear not, m'lord.

Then, I fear, your trunks and the university they contain must be sold, today, at auction.

Oh, Lord. I didn't say m'lord, Judge. I was invoking divine air, such as it is, or may be.

Doctor, there are many people here on our courthouse lawn. All trials in Virginia are open to the public. It is a bright and beautiful day. Bidding may be lively. Perhaps each book could be sold individually until the fare and the filing fee are recovered, and the remnant returned to you. You can find work here for a while and continue your odyssey of erudition.

Sir, my university is indivisible. All is interlocked, all is conjoined, all is ordered. Unlike a lizard, a skink, as I understand you Americans call them, do you know biology? My university cannot produce a new tail once a portion is bitten off. Sell all, including the trunks, and I will follow.

If that is your desire, Doctor. May Mr. Thompson conduct the auction?

Is he the man who announces the court?

Announces is not the word, but yes, Mr. Thompson, our clerk, calls and maintains our docket.

Aye, so best. I judge him a fair man.

We shall adjourn for 20 minutes, to allow those interested to examine the trunks and their contents. Then Mr. Thompson will call the auction. Mr. Nagotte, you shall have your $15 and the $2 filing *fee, and no more. Any balance goes to the doctor.*

Judge Russell retired to the courthouse. His countenance, it appeared to those who were there, was one of a man humorously enhanced, though respectful of the proceedings involving Dr. Wills.

Mrs. Green, I understand you wish to stand for the auction of Dr. Wills's glorious foundation, his traveling library.

Yes, sir.

Why?

Because, sir, I think Dr. Wills will follow his foundation to where it arrives—hopefully at Cherry Hill—and there, where it shall be sequestered in our library, for the Doctor's use, for the education of my son James Lewis, I mean, Buddy.

Have you funds for the purchase?

I have one silver plate, which was hidden in a chicken coop. The Yankees took all the chickens, and they found in the flower garden the spot where we had buried all the other silver. They had slim metal rods, Lord knows where they got them—all our iron metal was given to Richmond—and as they poked and poked and found and laughed when they found the silver. And said they would be rich. That silver came from England, but it is in the north now, I suppose.

What is that plate worth?

Sir, I do not know, in these times.

Judge Russell took the plate and examined it, turning back and forth in the sunlight.

We need to determine the value of this plate. By my eye it is 2 feet in diameter. I see Mr. Katz larking about in our crowd. Come up, Mr. Katz, and you shall be our expert witness today. For those who do not know Mr. Katz, he is from Warrenton and deals in gold, silver and sometimes rings, I think. He is fair, or relatively fair, I am told, in his dealings.

Katz approaches Judge Russell and takes the plate.

Examine it well, Mr. Katz., and give us a true value.

Katz takes the plate, turns it over and over, takes a spoon from a pocket in his vest, taps the plate in different places, places a glass from another pocket which fits against his eye and squints down.

It may be plated with silver. It has a cartouche with engraving in it, but the engraving is mostly worn away. I cannot say what it is or what it might say. It is not much tarnished, but it has seen much use.

How old, Mr. Katz?

I'd say between 200 and 250 years. Sometimes old give values, sometimes not.

What value, sir?

Maybe $40.

Mr Katz, did you see a clear lion passant on the plate?

I may have missed it.

I saw it, and I know what it means, by chance. You say the plate "may be plated with silver." A lion passant certifies the plate is sterling silver, that is 925 parts pure silver with 75 parts of copper to strengthen the plate for use. This plate is solid silver, not plated. The lion is stamped by the Bank of England. A judge makes findings of fact, based on evidence, especially the mark and, as here, his knowledge and good sense. I find as a fact this plate is worth $150. Who bids?

A dry goods merchant named Jamison bid $25.

That will not do. Other bids?

None were forthcoming.

Mr. Katz, you travel a circuit, as do I. That $25 is a local, a Culpeper, value. Your travels, I know, take you wider than mine, even to Washington, DC, and Baltimore, where this plate is worth much more than $150. I want you to make a profit. Thus, I accept your implied bid of $150. I noticed your heavy carpet bag when you exited the train this morning. Open it. That sum is to be paid in US silver dollars, immediately to Mrs. Green, and the plate is yours. Treat it carefully when you leave on the train. You have made a bargain, Mr. Katz, to your benefit. Mr. Thompson will verify the count.

Katz, wanting to return to future Rules Days, complied—and indeed to his profit in Baltimore.

We shall now auction Dr. Wills's "glorious foundation," including all trunks and bags containing his library. How to value books? They are but paper, vellum maybe, and glue. It is what they contain and how those contents are explained, presented, which is their true value. Bids?

I bid $50.

Other bids?

None were made.

Dr. Wills, the law gives you to right to match any bid and thus retain your property. Do you wish to bid?

M'lord—I'm sorry— your honor, I meant to say. I am skint. I have but $3 American to my name. I cannot match.

Other bids?

There were none.

Dr. Wills's property, as I have described it, goes to Mrs. Green. Mr. Thompson will deduct $17 for Mr. Nagotte. Doctor, the balance is yours—133 dollars. I know, as a Scot, you will spend, or rather, save it wisely. Mr. Thompson, please adjourn court.

Mrs. Green, where do you live?

Doctor, we live on a farm called Cherry Hill, near the hamlet of Amissville.

How do I get there? And can I please follow my library?

You have money now to complete your train ride, if you choose.

I follow my books, Dr. Wills said.

Then ride in my trap. It will take about an hour. And you will be most welcome at Cherry Hill—to stay and teach.

....

And thus Dr. Wills arrived at Cherry Hill. Where should he stay? It was the only bedroom on the first floor, and the largest in the house. All the rest were smaller and on the second floor. It had been occupied by Buddy's older siblings, two at a time, but the older ones had gone as they grew up, one to Fauquier County and one to Warren County, but the rest stayed in Culpeper.

Now it was used as a second parlor. And it was the warmest room in the house. It had its own fireplace and shared a wall with the kitchen and its wood burning stove. For many years, the children had been taught their letters and arithmetic there by their mother, and in turn, older siblings. There was in the barn a large slate board upon which writing and math problems had been inscribed.

And it had a library: the King James Version of the Bible, a complete Shakespeare, basic reading books for children, church tracts, *A History of Virginians for Virginians*, volumes of poems—Keats, Wordsworth, Longfellow, Shelley, Milton, Donne, Gray, two world geographies, biographies of Washington, Jefferson and Robert E. Lee, a copy of the Declaration of Independence and the United States Constitution, a map of the United States, and a map of Virginia, showing all the counties. All were owned by the Greens, accumulated and treasured, over many years.

And there were books from the lending library at the Amissville Methodist Church, which, surprisingly, contained some novels—James Fenimore Cooper, Hawthorne, Dickens, Melville. The Greens took turns reciting or reading parts, or all, of poems and of Shakespeare, mainly in the evening, surrounding a glowing kerosene lamp. And committing much to memory.

Now, there was also room on the shelves for parts of Dr. Wills's traveling library, on which Dr. Wills's books would rotate from his trunks to shelf and back again. Some parlor chairs were removed, the slate returned, and the room resumed its function as a school—for Buddy Green.

Dr. Wills was much pleased, as he feared he would be relegated to some outbuilding.

Now he had a feather bed in a comfortable room, The feather mattress was not new. When you lay down upon it, it squeezed down and the edges arose above one's head. The pillow, though, was new and firm. Wool blankets and towels were provided. And Dr. Wills was delighted to learn he would eat with the family.

3

Our lead, mined in Saxony in 58 B.C. and containing the isotope, was there smelted, and formed into lead bars. These bars were stored. In 47 B.C. eighty of these bars were transported by mule to Noviodunum (now Nevers, France) in Gaul located about 160 miles southwest of Paris, on the shores of the Loire River. Noviodunum, built in 52 B.C., was originally a supply depot for Roman soldiers and their auxiliaries. A large town developed around it, the population of which included many merchants. Our lead in Noviodunum was transformed into a pipe, about ten feet long and forty-eight inches from bottom to top. The lead was folded around a triangular wood frame and soldered together. It could weigh up to 850 pounds.

....

Dr. Wills was flattered to be considered one of the family, seated at the end of the table, with Mrs. Green at the other. Buddy, Eliza, Janie and Odessa were the only ones left at home, but often one or more of the older siblings would join for a meal. The table set usually for six, those in residence, though it could seat twelve, as circumstances required.

Dr. Wills learned to love roasted Guinea hen. He apprised the family that the name of the birds came from a place in Africa called Guinea, a fact unknown to the Greens, who had always thought they were native to America. He had never seen tomatoes actually growing, and often insisted on watering the plants. Succotash—a mixture of tomatoes, lima beans, corn and onions, heated in broth of chicken and butter —which he had never eaten, or even seen, became his special delight. He expanded his teaching duties to caring for the kitchen garden—planting, weeding, hoeing, watering all, but the tomatoes first. He called potatoes "tatties;" he called onions and other root vegetables "neeps" and always used those words, until the Greens knew what he was talking about, but they never used them. Mrs. Green's mashed potatoes—full of cream, butter, and pepper— were also a favorite. Roasted corn on the cob—butter, salt, and pepper—delighted him. Like succotash, he had never before eaten it in this form. Cherries and walnuts, gathered near the farmhouse, were abundant. The doctor's prayers for blackberry pie, after he first tasted one, were often answered. Especially on his birthday, October 7.

....

One night at dinner, Mrs. Green asked Buddy to say the children's prayer as the blessing.

He did: "God is great, God is Good, And we thank him for our Food. Amen."

Dr. Wills said: "God is nature." And no more than that. But Buddy remembered exactly what he had said. Thereafter, and as before, they honored the rule: "no politics or religion at the table." Except, of course, grace.

....

On his sixth birthday, his father gave Buddy a new rifle. Buddy had no idea how his father had acquired the money to purchase it. "I won a bet at the horse races," his father said.

The rifle was made by Remington Arms—.22 caliber, tubular magazine, which held fifteen shells, slide action to load each shell, semi-automatic. The barrel was thirty inches long, a very heavy hexagonal. It was stamped with a 1903 patent number. The rifle was deadly accurate at 100 yards. The bullet did not drop at that range. Buddy brought home squirrels, rabbits, and occasionally a sitting quail for the

kitchen. The family marveled at his accuracy. And Buddy
loved his rifle.

....

When Buddy was nine, his mother took him to the funeral
at Amissville Methodist for a boy his age who had died of
consumption after years of sickness. Buddy had known him
from Bible study for the children, held for a half hour after
services were completed. This time left the grown-ups to visit
one another. The boy's name was William Ledbetter. He lay in
a small coffin, with white clothes. He wore a white shirt with a
small black tie. His hands were resting on his chest. No tan
darkened his face.

His Mother said, "Look how smooth his hands are. He did
not need to work. And he is at rest now."

On the way home in the trap, he studied his hands—they
were calloused from his chores, and the interior of his left
hand had a scar all the way across just below his fingers. His
wood-carving knife had slipped when he had fallen, two years
ago. He was glad he had the scar. It proved he was alive.

....

Soon, Mrs. Green recognized that Dr. Wills needed spirits, as
had her late husband. Deprived, they acted the same—
nervous, wild-eyed, walking back and forth, jittery. She
wanted him to stay, to keep teaching Buddy, and she and the
children much liked him.

And so on each Rules Day and Market Day in Culpeper—
first and third Mondays—Morrison, the oldest of the children,
accompanied Mrs. Green, as often would the remaining
children from home.

Morrison had one duty: to buy spirits for Dr. Wills. Usually,
they were the water clear liquid that A. B. Cook, from
Warrenton, sold in quart jars from a wagon behind the Lord
Fairfax Hotel. But if funds permitted, they would buy two
quarts of the brown Bumgardner Rye, brought from the
Shenandoah Valley, over the mountains. They never missed a
Rules Day.

The first time she gave a quart jar of the clear liquid to Dr.

Wills, he appeared puzzled. But he took a sip, his face turned red, and he started to cry, silently, and slowly turned away, ashamed. Mrs. Green, embarrassed for him, smiled and walked away too.

Dr. Wills never again wanted for spirits. Buddy told his mother that he had a small square glass that he used to drink the spirits, which he kept on the top of the mantelpiece, behind a piece of what he called his tartan robe. The glass held what he called a "gill," about four ounces. He never drank except in his bedroom/schoolroom. And he only drank a gill, or perhaps two, on any day.

....

Dr. Wills liked geology and chemistry:

Buddy, you know the white hard rocks that surface in the lane, and hold up the corners of your house? They are quartz. Some of those old Greeks thought everything—you, me, trees, stones, fish—were made up of tiny invisible parts. A man named Liebnitz called them monads.

They are chemicals, or elements, though. A Frenchman named Lavorseiur figured out what oxygen was. It's what makes things burn. Put a burning candle under an upside-down glass jar and when the oxygen is gone the candle will go out. Fire needs oxygen to burn. You can try it and see.

That's an experiment. That's how we learn science, not to mention how to live. A Sassenach named Bacon said only experiments teach us how the world is put together.

Oh, what's a Sassenach? We Scots call the English that, but we do it quietly, and only when talking to other Scots.

Well those white rocks are composed of two chemicals: one called silicon and the other oxygen. Sand is part silicon. Somehow the two chemicals get merged, or mixed up together.

That's not quite true. The white comes from some other chemical to give it color. Some quartz is red, or blue or green. Some other chemical gives them their color. I don't know what chemicals give quartz color, but someone will figure it out. Pure quartz is made of two parts oxygen and one part silicon. And if they are the only two chemicals the quartz is clear, like the glass in a window or a jar.

We humans have no control over how that rock is put together. And, Laddie, that is something to remember. What control do we have over our lives? Not much, really. A Greek named Epictetus said that we should not worry, not fret, not even consider, matters over which we have no control. The only thing we can really control is how we live our lives. But how should we live our lives? That is a fundamental question. I wish I had an answer, a full answer, one that satisfied me. I think I have a part answer, I hope, for me. But everyone's answer will be different. It depends on their individual circumstances. Perhaps we shall talk about this sometime, but not now.

....

They were in the parlor, Buddy was fifteen. Dr. Wills said:

Lad, yes, Bobby Burns is wonderful. I am happy you like him—"tim'rous beastie." No, lad, not you, I know you are brave. Of the poets, and playwrights, I have to admit, there is none greater than Shakespeare, none with more wisdom, and heart. He was born down in England, but for him, there must always be an exception.

But we Scots—your mother told me both Greens and Woods have Scots blood. So you should be proud too. Like Wallace. I'll tell you about him one day. Great, great man. We Scots are solid cannie. We were "natural philosophers"—that's what they called scientists in the old days—not just wonderful poets.

I want to talk to you about those stones you find on that clay back path that leads up to the top of the hill behind that little building where we do our business.

James Hutton was an upland Scot, familiar with the islands up there. He went to the University of Edinburgh. Well, Hutton walked along the coast and visited the islands. It's mountains up there, mainly jagged, with some tall cliffs. In cliffs exposed to view, he saw they were in layers, like a cake with many layers, and with different colors and different thickness and different hardness. Some layers were curved up, some down, in places, and some not curved at all. He found some layers, way up high, that had fossils—small fish-like creatures, hardened to stone, in different layers—above and below the more hardy layers he knew were granite like.

How did they get there? They weren't like modern fishes. And when and how did they get there. He knew volcanos, or earthy eruptions, made mountains. And some mountains were sharp, jagged, and some were gentle, smoother, like around Edinburgh.

He reasoned that the world was much older than people thought. That each layer got thrust up sometime, and later layers also thrust up, all over millions of years. And that the layers with fish like creatures must have been in the bottom of the sea at one point. Look! I have a fossil. I got it in Edinburgh. It's one of those fishes, sort of curled up. In this piece of black slate, somehow turned into stone. The slate was probably mud. It was once on the bottom of some sea.

Now, the reason some mountains were jagged, and some smoother, was the smoother ones had been worn down, like round pebbles on the beach, or in a river or stream, while the jagged mountains were newer. It was rain, and wind, which must wear a jagged mountain into a smooth mountain. And it takes a long, long time to wear down a jagged mountain. Those Blue Ridge mountains to the west are old. Look at them. They are not ragged, like the Rocky Mountains I have seen in pictures.

Hutton wrote all this down in a journal of natural philosophy and many cannie doctors teaching at universities read it. He had discovered what he called "deep time." And most of the other natural philosophers said he was right. All over England and even in Europe. He did this over 200 years ago. He thought and he wrote. Thought precedes action, as lightning precedes thunder. Remember that: first think—then act.

A fool named Bishop Ussher—English of course—figured out from the Bible that God made the world on October 19, at 9 o'clock, on 4004 B.C. He didn't say whether it was 9 in the morning, or 9 at night. It's jolly fun to remember that name and date. Hutton put an end to that insanity.

Well, to continue, another Scot, Joseph Black, said atoms, the little parts of everything, can join together. And a scientist named John…. I tartle…. John Dalton—I have to admit he was English, though he was part Irish, which is probably where he got his brain parts. He said atoms of different elements, or chemicals, and different weights, can fuse together, in different proportions but mathematical proportions, to form the rocks we see. And everything else in the world. They figured this out about eighty years ago. Nobody knows how the atoms hook together, but one day we will learn. Last time I heard, and it was fifteen years ago, they had deciphered twenty-four elements. If I remember correctly they included copper, silicon, sulfur, mercury, phosphorus, gold, and lead. I guess they have found more since then.

That's how I told you about the white quartz. Like those stones you find in the clay, they are crystals. But they are not quartz. The ones you dig up are square or rectangular. They are like tarnished yellow, or shiny brown, in color golden. They have, or had, perfect right angles.

Sometimes they are stacked up on one another, not straight, but twining. But each still has right angles. I have seen crystals with six sides, with eight sides, all with equal angles too. Somehow, the atoms lock together, perfectly, and add up, in accordance with mathematics. They are ordered somehow. The ones you find on the surface—their angles are not sharp, some of those stones are almost rounded. They are like the mountains. Worn down by rain, wind, and tumbling.

You and I know there is iron in those stones, because they stick to my magnet. There is another element, or maybe more, in them. I don't know what. But they fit together in an orderly manner.

Neither the Doctor or Buddy knew, but the stones were iron pyrites, one atom of sulphur and two atoms of iron. Known as Fool's Gold.

……………

Our lead, now part of a pipe, was purchased by Arrius Tullia, of Noviodunum. He was of mixed Roman and Germanic blood, and was a rich grain merchant in wheat and barley. In 28 A.D., Tullia had built a home on a hill along the shores of the Loire, with an atrium, a bath, and toilets. Waste water flowed down through a lead pipe buried, containing our lead isotope, into the Loire.

....

On June 24, 1916, the Culpeper Star-Exponent published the following statement by the Democratic National Re-Election committee, in support of President Wilson's campaign: "The Democratic administration has throughout the present war scrupulously and successfully held to the old paths of neutrality...."

On April 2, 1917, President Wilson asked a joint session of Congress for a declaration of war against the German Empire.

On April 6, 1917, Congress did so.

....

Surprisingly, on a Sunday morning, Dr. Wills, after many declined and now ended entreaties, agreed to go to Amissville Methodist Church. He had long before been repeatedly assured the Methodists were definitely Protestant.

The Bible reading came from Proverbs 22:9: "The generous themselves will be blessed for they share their food with the poor." The sermon spoke of the redeeming grace of charity. Dr. Wills was glad there was no kneeling, no touching the chest, no counting beads, no Papist gestures.

Later that same day, in the parlor where much of the family sat, Dr. Wills said:

Your church is not unlike the Kirk in Scotland. That is what we call our church. I liked the hymn. I had never heard it before, "A mighty Fortress Is Our God." And I like what the minister said. Charity, I believe, is the most precious trait. And like the Bible reading, particularly like the reading. You Greens have fed the poor. And I shall never forget your charity.

But Dr. Wills never again attended church, and Mrs. Green never urged him to do so, for she sensed, correctly, that Dr.

Wills would decline, as before.

That night, in bed, Mrs. Green, just prior to saying her prayers, remembered another Bible quotation: "Do not neglect to show hospitality to strangers, for thereby some have entertained angels unaware." Hebrews 13:2.

Somehow, she thought, and, perhaps, Dr. Wills.

....

The Schafferchutzen-Gewehr 98. The German sniper rifle built with adjustable sights and telescopic scope, developed in 1893. Made by Mauser. 5 round internal clip, Mauser bullets— lead steel jacketed. 7.92 X 57 mm. Range up to 1200 yards.

....

Despite being an English tradition, Dr. Wills loved tea. The Greens could afford English tea only during the Christmas season. Coffee was never in their budget. What tea did they usually drink? Sassafras, though it was called "Indian Tea"— because the Indians had invented it in ages past. Sassafras bushes, small trees really, were abundant. One took the roots, scraped off the tender bark, splintered it, and steeped it in boiling water. It turned from darkish red, to brown, as it strengthened. Its flavor came from scafrole oil embedded in the bark, though that fact was unknown to those who drank it. The tea was naturally sweet and sometimes it was further sweetened with honey. It was supposed to aid in curing certain ailments—stomach problems, gout—but that was country fantasy. Dr. Wills came to accept it, with pleasure, over the years.

....

One day, Buddy found in the spinner and yellow gorse behind the barn an odd piece of stone, half buried. It had been hewn, obviously. Examining it, he discerned it was a part of a circle, with part of a small hole in the bottom. The circle would have had a diameter of about five feet. Later that day, he asked his mother if she knew what it was. She told him it was a part of a grindstone, a round piece of stone that sat upright, vertically, in a frame with a wooden handle and a crank. You turned it around and around to sharpen tools—sickles, axe heads, knives. It had broken when she was a little girl and thrown away. Now such tools were sharpened by a man named Tublecain, from Warrenton, who traveled on Rules Days to local towns, a mechanism for sharpening bolted to the bed of his wagon.

Several days later, Buddy asked Dr. Wills about the stone. He was told:

It is sandstone. Remember Hutton—limestone was in the layers in the mountains he saw. It is formed when the shells of tiny creatures on the bottom of the sea get raised up, and then pressed down from above and heated up from below. They become chalk, soft, like we use on the board. Chalk becomes sandstone, in turn, if you keep pressing and heating the chalk. And sandstone, heated and pressed again, becomes limestone, and with more heat and pressure it becomes marble. It is a marvelous transformation. But it takes millions of years. You know the bowl your Mother has, to hold sugar? It is marble. The red splotches in it are caused by other minerals mixed in. Probably iron. Somehow the minerals interlock, tighten, and get smoother and harder. We know it starts with the shells; the shells are made of calcium, like, I think, our bones and teeth. We don't know what other element, or probably elements, are added. But we know there must be something added, along the way.

Buddy kept the piece of grindstone to sharpen his knife.

....

One day, Buddy initiated the conversation:

You once said, Doctor, and I remember it exactly: "God is nature." But that was all. Is that what the natural philosophers thought?

Dr. Wills:

Protestants, Papists, Jews, Mohamedans, the old Greeks and Romans, and even those Asian religionists have the same idea, but differently jumbled up: that there is a god, or gods, that look down on us from somewhere and care about and sometimes direct or stymie our actions; that each sent us earthly messengers to tell us what God wants or demands; and that there is an afterlife for us, for some in their heaven, for some in their hell. I think they are all wrong. Don't misunderstand me—I liked your church. It was very nice, and so were the people there. Now, I must admit that the Kirk in Scotland may be my fallback, my retreat, when the time comes, just in case. But I don't think I will ever retreat.

I wasn't the first to say, or think, that God is Nature. 500 years ago a man named Spinoza, a Jewish Dutch man, wrote that. They threw him out of his church, his synagogue, for saying it. He thought that the world is put together in a manner that is orderly, that nature is orderly, and that that order was God, and that therefore God was Nature. I think he was right. Consider: you and I, and everything in the world, your stones, the trees, the grass, your mare, Blackie, the clouds, water, food, my dose of spirits, are made up of chemicals, or elements, or atoms. They are put together differently, but always in an orderly manner. And those chemicals have existed for all time, for the deep time in the past, as Hutton found, and will exist for all time in the future. And thus we, you and I, always have been and always will be part of the order.

Nature's order. God's order. That should console us.

A long pause.

I care greatly for you, Buddy. You have an amazing memory, and that is good, at times. You have memorized so much of the Bible and Shakespeare, it is amazing. Thank your Mother. And you are as smart as paint. You listen, always, to my babble, and I think with respect, and perhaps with memory. That respect, and memory, is very, very endearing to me. It makes my life…. I fear I have grown tired. Quite tired. And so off to bed for me. Goodnight.

Buddy did not see the tears that had developed in Dr. Wills's eyes.

....

The lead pipe served the Tullia family home for three generations, and a second family, named Devereaux, for three generations more. The former had named the home "Hill Domun" or "Hill House" in English. In 187 A.D., the Aedui, an ancient Celtic tribe, revolted, as the Roman wall of protection had long decayed on the frontiers of Gaul. They captured Noviodunum, killed all men, took the women and children into slavery, and burnt the town, which was abandoned.

....

Buddy loved the spring at the bottom of the hill. He paused there, often for hours, resting from his travels up and down to the farmhouse, with the two buckets waiting re-filling. Many times, Dr. Wills would accompany Buddy on this duty, likewise carrying two buckets, slacking the pace, however, with his carefully calculated slower steps.

The spring water itself bubbled from up under a large red oak, surrounded by forest, beside a stream—a stream of about a one half foot depth—and with timeless and constant flow the spring added to the water the stream provided. At this juncture, a basin had been dug, a partial circle, three feet in truncated circumference, two feet deep, at some unknown time by a Green in the past. The downstream side of the basin was dammed with a combination of rocks, as closely fitted as their shapes allowed, and clay. Through this dam was inserted a small copper pipe, long aged green, through which the level of the encompassed water was regulated and maintained, the outlet calibrated, through experience by some Green ancestors. By the side of the basin had been placed a flat sandstone slab, upon which you could kneel while filling your buckets. A rusty trowel lay beside the stone, for mending the clay in the dam and clearing the bottom of the basin, so the accumulated water level lowered to its designed depth. The basin was shaded, which offered a portion of protection from evaporation, even at high summer.

The stream itself arose somewhere to the west, its origin unknown. Backtracking out of curiosity for a mile or so, Buddy found it nearly straight, tumbling downwards through a series of rock-bound minor gorges, in miniature waterfalls, sometimes gathering in small pools, and then outwards again, toward its merger with the spring, and thence contributing, several miles later, to the much larger Indian Run.

Downstream of the basin, the stream widened, bordered by even flat grassy areas, each about 20 feet in breadth, for close to 35 yards, with coiled fern fronds of different species adorning the stream-sided edges, generated both by the sun and the fracture in the surrounding forest.

As the stream widened, gravity diminished its velocity, creating gravel fans. Here grasses bent and bowed in the flow. Here grew wild watercress, to be gathered in season, to augment salads.

He would remember, most devotedly, those trips to the spring with Dr. Wills.

....

Buddy's mother possessed a sharp wit, and one infused with phrases, almost unconsciously, from the Bible and Shakespeare, each of which she read by a kerosene lamp almost nightly. That wit, her intense intelligence, her profound memory, her logical mind, all were used for direction, praise, and admonition. If the latter, the family knew a storm might arise if she said, "Don't stir up my Irish temper." Her maiden name—Jane Anna Wood, certainly not an Irish surname—with this designation was never challenged, for, if so, the storm would surely rise. And she could tell a story, spell binding, one remembered or of her composition, and she told one many evenings to her children, after their prayers, entrancing them as they lay in bed, awaiting sleep.

The Greens were poor, but never crushed by poverty. They had immense pride and steadfast faith, in their family, in learning, in hard work, in their religion, in Virginia, and in Cherry Hill.

Buddy's mother had taught, and most ably, the girls and Buddy to read, write, and do mathematics, as she had been taught as a child by her mother. She was a stern and relentless teacher and her efforts were rewarded. They were required to read all books in the family library, and recite from memory selected portions of Shakespeare or of poems. The girls and Buddy were more proficient than had they been taught in the public school in the town of Culpeper.

After her husband died, the chores of running the farm rested on Jane and her four children. Morrison Green was always willing to help Cherry Hill, and though Jane Wood

Green was only his step-mother, her children were of his blood. And he loved them all. Cherry Hill would not have remained in the family but for his generous and continuous efforts.

Initially, though, only Eliza, Odessa, and Janie, born in that order, could aid her. James Lewis was too young. The duties, depending upon their weight and complexity, increased with the girls' ages.

Those duties were based upon the seasons, and the necessity those seasons compelled: bring water up the hill from the spring, for drink and cooking; transfer water from the rain barrels for washing bodies and clothes; prepare, plant, water, hoe, protect, and gather the plants in the kitchen garden; tend the horses; collar and prepare a Guinea hen for cooking; snap string beans, shuck corn, peel potatoes and mash them, can summer produce; gather eggs from the chicken coop; fill kerosene lamps; sew tattered clothes; make beds, empty chamber pots, and most onerous of all—split rounds of wood for use in the kitchen stove and fireplaces, and stack those splits, the oldest and driest, on the small covered porch adjacent to the kitchen. The splitting required the insertion of iron pins in the rounds, to aid the splitting by the maul, to augment the strength required.

With Morrison Green's aid, her stepson and Mrs. Green directed employed traveling farm workers as to the planting and later harvesting and storing in the barn, for later transportation to the silos of Amissville, the grains of the fields of Cherry Hill. The crops were primarily corn, with some wheat.

....

Morrison loved Buddy, and acting as his mentor following their father's death, continued his education in the arts of men. How to defend your honor; how to ride and care for a horse; how to devastatingly fight and surely wound an opponent; how to track an animal, how to read the signs of the seasons and the foresight of the skies; and most diligently—and with foresight and consequences presently unknown—how to be an excellent shot.

....

But the duty, though not so considered by the girls, was aiding their mother at cooking. They considered that duty rather a joy—collecting, cutting, measuring, timing and tending the stove—and listening to the recipes that their mother methodically recited, committing them to memory, sometimes writing the more complex ones on scraps of paper.

All the girls had light brown hair, and either blue or hazel eyes, with skin clear and pure, bodies strong, slim, and willowy. Eliza grew to be the tallest, a surprising 5 feet 7 inches, while Janie and Odessa each were 5 feet 4.

When their little brother arrived, and grew, the girls duties became increasingly lightened.

Buddy's first duties involved aiding the girls in the kitchen garden, and progressively increased. By the time he was twelve, some became solely his—carrying the water up from the spring in the buckets and splitting and stacking the wood —dried to the porch, recently split to barn. His schooling was the same as his siblings had been, by his mother, though his older sisters refined it. He became even more proficient than they, having the serendipitous arrival of a stranger from Scotland.

By the time he was seventeen, his growth ceased. He was 5 feet 9 inches, wiry, and quite strong. His hair is light brown. His eyes are hazel. He little by little replaced Morrison in the onerous requirements of Cherry Hill, with the experienced Morrison guiding him.

4

In 1914, when Buddy was sixteen, Dr. Wills died. It was a Friday. He had not answered his mother's call for breakfast. She found him lying on his side, in his nightshirt, next to the bookshelves. There was a full gill in the glass on the bedside table. He somehow looked peaceful, his countenance gentle, his eyes closed. They never knew his exact age.

Over the years, he had given Buddy all but one of his silver dollars, the vestige of the sale of his library in Culpeper, to be passed on to Mrs. Green. Buddy, of course, had done so, noting their provenance.

Where should he be buried? Buddy spoke up:

He would not like a church yard. He used to walk with me down to the spring. He would even carry a bucket to help me tote the water up the hill. Many times he said how beautiful the flowing water was, coming into and out of the spring, from the creek. I always had to wait, because he would sit very still with his eyes shut for a time. Once he said he could hear the water gently rumbling. Once he said God was here. I think he should be buried just down from the spring, next to the creek. He never told us of any family back in Scotland. So we have no one to tell of his death.

Dr. Wills had been living at Cherry Hill for almost seven years. He had become in the united view of the Greens a member of their family—a treasured, and indeed, loved member.

It was agreed—the spring. They knew Buddy knew Dr. Wills best, that he would choose a proper location for his grave. He had spent so many hours with him.

The next day, Rules Day in Culpeper, they bought a pine coffin, the only kind they could afford. Morrison dressed him in the suit Wills had worn when he went to Amissville Methodist Church that one time. He had never worn it before, or after. They added the piece of his tartan robe, and his remaining silver dollar.

The next morning, after dressing, but before heading for church, they trundled a cart holding the coffin down the hill to the spring and the stream. Buddy had dug the grave there, the day preceding.

Eliza placed some daffodils on the coffin. Buddy put the last shovel full on the top of the grave. No one prayed out loud, but all, silently, said their chosen prayer. All were crying, quietly.

Buddy was asked to speak.

He remembered part of a poem from the parlor library—Gray's "Elegy in a Country Churchyard"—and Dr. Wills's belief. He recited:

Ev'n from the tomb the voice of nature cries Ev'n in our ashes live their wonton fires.

They walked, slowly, up the hill to the house. No one spoke.

Buddy's crying returned, that night, in bed, after he said his prayers. He could not stop, crying softly as the murmuring of a spring. Nonetheless, he pulled his pillow over his face, hoping to muffle the sound.

Adjacent to the lane leading to the county road were large distorted and jagged pieces of white quartz—though the ordered structure of the crystals within remained. Over the years they had been removed and cast aside to ease passage. A month after Dr. Wills' death, Buddy chose one, unblemished by another color. He spent two days with a hammer and chisel slowly knapping it into a cube, a hexahedron, of equal dimensions of fifteen inches on all six sides. The exterior remained course, but one would recognize it as distinctly defined, shaped, by man. On a trip down to the spring Buddy put this structure in one of the buckets, and placed it on Dr. Wills' grave.

....

On March 2, 1918, a postcard (Form 1011) from the War Department arrived at the Post Office in Jeffersonton, Culpeper County, Virginia. It was addressed to James Lewis Green. The postmaster in Jeffersonton was named Lucas Whitehead. The office was part of his country store. He knew no James Lewis Green. An old man, a Confederate veteran, named Randolph Evans, entered to buy some Mail Pouch chewing tobacco.

Randy, I don't know any Greens around here. Do you?

No, but there are a bunch of Greens at Amissville and thereabouts.

Whitehead scratched out "Jeffersonton" and wrote in pencil "Amissville, Virginia" on the postcard. He forwarded it.

The postcard read:

You are hereby notified that you have been found...qualified for military service which leaves you in Class 1a, subject to call in your order of call when the Government may have need of your service.

The postcard arrived at Cherry Hill on March 5, 1918.

Suppose Evans had not walked in the store at that moment. And suppose Whitehead had written on the same: Not deliverable at the address designated? And returned it to sender?

That would have ended the matter. Purely random this occurrence, as was the creation of the isotope lead 88 in our lead. And we would not be writing, as we shall, about the Meuse-Argonne in October. Purely random, or somehow ordered?

* * *

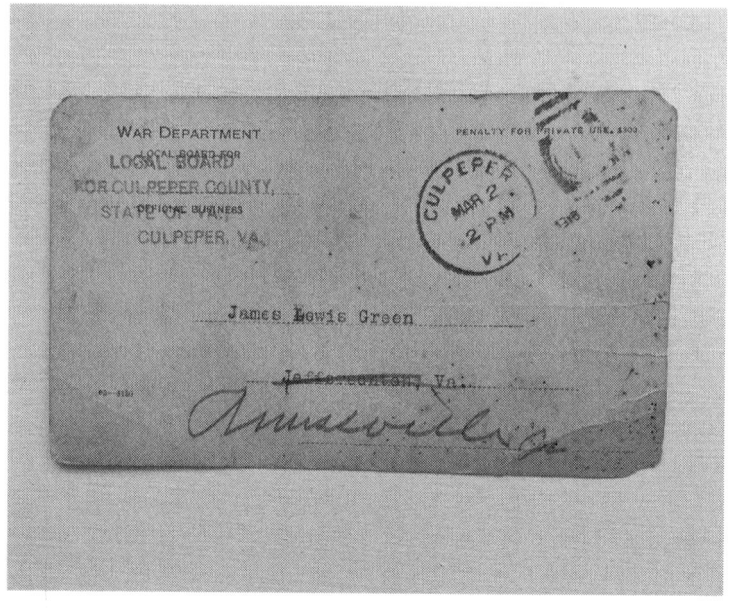

WAR DEPARTMENT
LOCAL BOARD
FOR CULPEPER COUNTY,
STATE OFFICIAL BUSINESS
CULPEPER, VA.

PENALTY FOR PRIVATE USE, $300

James Lewis Green

....

The lead pipe remained buried in the banks of the Loire for over 200 years. The flooding Loire in 395 A.D. undercut the bank on which the remains of Hill House sat; and that debris, and our lead pipe, collapsed into the Loire and was covered by the flowing and burying silt. There it remained for almost 1,500 years—its existence buried likewise.

....

One beautiful Sunday, blue-sky day, June 7, 1918, he saw a girl he had never seen before, after services at the church, as he mingled with the adults. He was nineteen. After introducing himself, she told him her name was Ann Davis. He knew that was a Welsh name, from Dr. Wills, though her voice had an Irish tilt.

She carried a basket, its contents covered by a white napkin. She said it was a picnic lunch for herself and her younger sister. But that sister had not, at the last minute, joined her, as she was "indisposed." A cousin, some family in Culpeper he did not know, was to escort her back to Richmond.

She invited him to share, inquiring if there were a shaded place to eat it.

Below the church, about forty-five yards downhill, ran a clear stream—a tributary of the Rapidan—which traversed a meadow, bubbling over rounded stones, bordered by white oaks. Buddy suggested it as a venue, and she agreed. It seemed she walked as delicately as a kitten on fallen snow.

She was wearing a blue dress, of silken material, just below knee length, with sleeves ending mid-arm. She was slender, but tall for a girl, almost 5 feet 6. She had reddish blond hair, at shoulder length, snow-white skin, summer tanned, hazel eyes, and a thin saddle of freckles over her nose and under her eyes. The lovely shape of her lips. The curl of her ear. Buddy thought he had never seen a woman so beautiful. She was seventeen.

Both seated, she produced ham and cheese sandwiches, and a container of what was lemonade, two cups he recognized as silver, all placed on the white napkin, spread on the grass between them, in the shade of an enormous white oak.

Upon his enquiries, he learned, increasingly fascinated:

Her father was a surveyor for the Commonwealth. They had stayed the night before in the Lord Fairfax Hotel in Culpeper on their way to Sperryville, down the Sperryville road to the west. Her father was to survey some mountains which rose above that town. It was a summer family excursion. They too were Methodists and had stopped at Amissville Methodist to break up their travel.

Their family lived in Richmond; she attended a real school for girls there, called the Orchard School. She was going off to college that fall, to a school called Sweetbriar, in a town over the mountains in the Valley. She was to study English.

He thought perhaps he asked too many questions and apologized, but she just smiled and said she was flattered he did so. His answers to her reciprocal questions were limited, for his experiences, he felt, were necessarily narrow, too much to do with farming, with the country, not a city; a home he knew would not compare to hers, his life too plain, next to hers. But she listened with apparent intensity, graciously.

The conversation turned to literature. He described what he had read, noting all she might deem worthwhile—Shakespeare, poets, some novels—in the parlor library. He thought, somehow, he had to prove himself, to demonstrate he was not unlearned.

He recited Shakespeare's Sonnet 18:

Shall I compare thee to a summer's day? Thou art more lovely and more temperate:

Rough winds do shake the darling buds of May, And summer's lease has all too short a date; Sometime too hot the eye of heaven shines, And often is his gold complexion dimmed;

And every fair from fair sometime declines,

By chance or nature's changing course untrimm'd; But thy eternal summer shall not fade,

Nor lose possession of that fair thou ow'st;

Nor shall death brag thou wander'st in his shade, When in eternal lines to time thou grow'st:

So long as men can breathe or eyes can see, So long lives this, and this gives life to thee

Her eyes widened. Her face, radiant, presented a smile. She raised her hands, upright as in prayer, and silently applauded. Buddy blushed.

But then the conversation turned to music—she talked of Handel, of Mozart—of whom he had never heard. He knew hymns from church, and Scots-Irish songs that Morrison sometimes sang—but it ended there. Again, he felt shame. To this he could not intelligently respond.

He could not take his eyes off Ann. Her narrow ankles and slender legs, the tiny golden hairs on her tanned arms, the swell of her chest, her scent—it seemed a mixture of honeysuckle, of the fragrance of broken stems of the tiger lilies that surrounded the house at Cherry Hill, of roses.

They exchanged addresses, promising to write, but he never knew if she had, as soon he would no longer be at Cherry Hill.

He was entranced, totally, by Ann Davis, in a manner he had never before felt. Her beauty and brilliance overwhelmed him, encompassing him. He would never forget her.

....

On June 10, 1918, the telegram, actually a pencil-written copy, arrived by messenger at Cherry Hill. At that time, there were no typewritten copies of messages on Western Union forms. Once deciphered from the dots and dashes, the message was transcribed on whatever scrap of paper was available. Messages were delivered by teenagers, wearing a Western Union shirt, thus identified, to the designated recipient, by foot or horse. This message read:

Greetings from the President of the United States...You are ordered to appear at the Courthouse in Culpeper, Virginia, on June 15 at 1 p.m. You have been called to active service in the armed forces of the United States. Adjutant General, U.S. Army.

It was five days away. Buddy wondered: what will they do with me? Where will they send me? His mother:

Probably France. They said at church that was where they were sending our Army.

Buddy went to the parlor and studied the world atlas map of Europe, trying to learn of the geography of that country, France.

His Mother told him:

Don't wear good clothes. They'll give you some.

So Buddy wore some tattered old overalls, a blue flannel shirt, almost white socks, and his father's abandoned high-top shoes—he put cardboard from a box of canning jars to cover the holes in the shoes. She prepared two chicken sandwiches, wrapped in grease paper, for his trip.

His mother, crying, could not bring herself to take Buddy; his oldest half brother, Morrison Green, drove him into town in his trap.

When he arrived, he was met by an old sergeant in uniform, standing on the courthouse lawn. There was no one else there his age, waiting. The sergeant produced a Bible, King James Version, and swore Buddy into service. They waited almost two hours, silently, when a truck arrived. It had been to Warrenton. There were fourteen Virginians aboard.

They traveled through a town Buddy had never seen—Richmond—Ann Davis's home. From Richmond through Hampton, where Buddy got a glimpse of the ocean he also had never before seen. They passed marshy inlets, satiated by estuarial streams, choked with viridian sea willows, shaggy seagulls circling above.

The truck had nattered along, fitfully, for two and a half hours, until it arrived at a gate, where a sentry box and two armed soldiers guarded the entrance.

Above the gate was a sign: Welcome to Camp Lee, Virginia. It was June 16, 1918.

He was part of the 155th Depot Brigade, though he never heard that designation.

Camp Lee had been hurriedly, and shabbily, built in 1917, in Prince George County. There were wooden barracks and large tents—barely enough space for the draftees—a mess hall, storage buildings, four wells, and a magazine bunker. A row of outhouses, and latrine trenches, behind each barrack or tent. The tarpaper barracks roofs constantly leaked.

The camp had been designated a "mobilazational camp." The soil was sandy—only spare pine trees—and the climate humid, semi-tropical. Some days the searing sunlight was as sharp as a straight razor. At night the camp was lit by floodlights, aswarm with insects, tracing v-shaped patterns in the darkened sky.

Buddy was given a physical, a haircut, and issued two olive green utility uniforms —tunic, pants, three undershirts, three underwear, three pairs of socks, a slouch hat—and new boots. It was the first pair of new shoes he had ever had. They threw away the clothes he arrived in, but let him keep his blue flannel shirt. He also got two towels, three pieces of carbide soap, a razor, a toothbrush, a canteen, a tin cup, a mess kit with a spoon/knife combination.

The draftees were taught to march, to obey basic commands, put through a series of physical exercises, and taught to use a bayonet, against straw-filled bags. And on the third day of camp, tests to see if they could read and write and do basic mathematical calculations. The lessons in the parlor, taught by his Mother and older siblings, before Dr. Wills arrived, came to the fore. He was told he was "most proficient" and his ability would be noted in his military record. This ability was never referred to again. He was amazed that so many that so many of his fellow draftees could do neither, had no such ability.

And, relentlessly, they were marched to the rifle range.

There they learned how to strip down the rifle for cleaning, and how to quickly re-assemble it; how to load the clips with bullets; how to adjust the sites; how to fire, sitting, standing, prone; how to approximate the distance to the targets. The targets were hogsheads barrels, butts with white paper targets affixed.

The rifle was a 1903 Springfield, made at the Springfield Armory, starting in that year. It was 30.06 caliber, bolt action, with a five-round clipper strip inserted from below, and forty-four inches long. Supposedly accurate at 1,100 yards, but actually only about 800. The fire rate, which the sergeants repeatedly yelled must be met, had to be twenty rounds of shots per minute. No one could fire, eject, and load four clips in that time.

Buddy noted that 1903 was the same year as his Remington at home. And his accuracy he learned with that rifle was demonstrated with his target practice. The teaching sergeant named him a "sharpshooter."

He was from Alabama and said:

Boy, you could shoot the red off a blackbird's wing.

He was given a small red tag with sharpshooter designation, and it was sewn on his tunic.

It went into his military record, and it was to be noted in France.

....

On Knights of Columbus stationery, labeled "War Activities":
June 25, 1918.
Dear Mother and All
I arrived here safe about 10 days ago.

They have me so busy running around I could not before write. They give you paper and envelopes for free, and you don't have to buy a stamp. You live in tents, or barracks, with a bunch of other guys who got called up. I have met several guys from Virginia, many from over the mountain in the valley. And some from towns around Richmond. But none in my barracks.

There are guys from North Carolina too. And a sergeant, regular Army, who runs the show. He too lives in our barracks, but he has a room for himself. He is a Yankee and sometimes I can't understand what he says.

As you predicted they gave me clothes, and new boots that almost fit. They let us wash in something called a "shower" which is metal with holes in it above your head, and the water drips down. No tubs. It is like the rain, when I would wash in the summer at home. The food is not too bad, some things I have never eaten, and do not even know what they are or are called. They don't taste bad. But there is plenty of food.

This place is really hot, a kind of wet hot, and the mosquitoes eat you alive.

I have to close now because we are set to do "physical exercise"—jumping up and down, lying down and sitting up, and other contortions, and running. Will write again as soon as I can. I feel so lonesome I could cry, but that would not be what soldiers do, I guess.

Your loving son and brother, Buddy

....

On Army and Navy Young Men's Christian Association stationery, labeled "With the Colors":
July 1, 1918
Dear Mother and all,

I read your letter and was real glad to hear from you all. We are quarantined because of some sickness and can't get out of the barracks and we are about as thick as one can stand. They let us out sometimes to go to the rifle range, but it is so hot and we go without any breakfast or dinner. I have been run around like a headless Guinea hen here, doing what they tell me. They are always yelling.

It is bad here, but I know it is better than when we get to the other side. I have a horror of going across. Well it hurts to think about it. See if you can sell Blackie and the colt, and if you cant trade her and the colt for a good cow. She will be too old when I get back, if I ever do. Also, give my Remington to Morrison because he taught me to do many things, and he always helped at Cherry Hill, even when he had his own place to worry about.

Give my love to Eliza and Odessa and all the others. If I get killed, you will get the insurance which they say is $10,000. From the Army or the U.S. government. I cant imagine that much money.

I love all of you.

Buddy

....

On Knights of Columbus stationery, labeled "War Activities":
July 6, 1918
Dear Mother and all of you.

I don't have much time to write. I have been vaccinated twice to protect from sickness you can get when you get over there. I guess that is a good thing. I don't know whether I will get back or not.

Some of the officers are pretty good and some are as mean and rough as they can be. They say toughness is for our good, so we will be tough over there. I don't see how yelling at you helps.

It is so hot that when you go to the mess hall you have to hold your nose because of spoiled food they throw out back. And the mosquitoes will eat you alive. Thank goodness they don't much like the colder weather at home.

You asked me in your letter what I would take for Blackie and the colt. I think $40 for Blackie alone, and $75 for both. If you can't do any better, I guess you should take $35 for Blackie because she is hard to winter. Make the buyer pay in silver dollars rather than in the new Federal paper money. Silver dollars will always be worth something.

I wish I could come home and visit. They won't let us leave here, and I won't get home until the war is over. I might be dead then. I hope they will ship my body back. At least I will be home again.

Orders came in, and the rumors say we leave here sometime soon to go to France. I think several thousand of us. We are supposed to go on a train to New York City to get on a boat. I am very afraid to go across. But I will do my best. The sergeants make us yell and sing war songs. I don't know what good that does. I have had only a month of training and I am not sure that is enough to be a good soldier. I should not say it, I guess, but most of the training seems worthless. You're supposed to learn more in battle, I fear.

My rifle, the Springfield 1903, can shoot a long way and when you do the bolt back and forth you can fire five bullets before reloading. It's about time to turn off the lights in our barracks. I never mentioned before but they have electricity here, like in Culpeper. But the glass jars often burn out and there is no light until you put a new one in. No kerosene lamps.

Please go to the church and say prayers for me. I dont want to go because I think I will be killed over there, I don't know why I think that, and I wish I didn't. But I cant get it out of my mind. I won't have any use for horses or anything else. I have a horror of going across.

Goodbye to you all, and goodbye to Virginia.

Your loving Buddy, and brother in Christ

5

They were loaded on open trucks and traveled on to the Norfolk train yards. There sixty replacements were assigned to each passenger car—designed to hold thirty people. The toilet at the end was locked, not for use.

A Regular Army sergeant controlled each car. The train—Richmond, Fredericksburg and Potomac—chugged trough Richmond on to Potomac Yards, in Alexandria, Virginia, across the Potomac River. They were told to exit the cars, the Sergeant counted each man off and kept them together in a group, a stern shepherd. They were told now was the time to urinate or evacuate, for they would be using the same cars, which would be on a parallel track, six tracks away. Anyone trying to get away would be immediately shot, the sergeant warned.

They waited for two hours while the passenger cars were "humped"—pushed up a ramp and sent down—to be hooked on a different track, to be attached to a waiting, panting, New York Central engine. They were counted again as they entered.

That engine pulled them through Baltimore to Philadelphia, where it idled gently chugging, while coal and water were replenished. Thence, on through New Jersey, through that portion called the "Pine Barrens," car couplers jostling, passing waste lands and stagnant pools of water, shimmering with sheathings of wayward oil, and finally across a bridge over the East River, into Grand Central Station. They were counted again, and assembled on the platform.

....

They were marched down 2nd Avenue, nine men abreast at double time, to its intersection with 25th Street, where stood the Armory of New York's 69th regiment. Blazing in the heat, the square building was concrete, and the texture of its walls was unevenly highlighted by an accumulation of the greasy brownish-yellow residue of coal-smoke and salt-laden air from the river to the east. The botching reminded Buddy of the markings on a copperhead snake. The building's windows were severely narrow, almost like arrow ports, and those on the first floor, narrower yet, were protected with inset vertical bars of steel. The command to halt was given.

The ranks were slowly divided by the sergeants, whose commands were either misunderstood or never before heard by the men, and so with difficulty were three lines of two men abreast finally established, and then with continued confusion positioned one man placed behind another. With curses tinged with amazement the sergeants mutually reinforced their uniform view that these men were not even trained to march. The platoons and companies mixed, and every soldier was now a stranger to those beside him, and to those before and behind him.

Each soldier stumbled lonely through a narrow half oval entrance to the Armory, over which hung, gargoyle-like, an Iblisian bronze eagle, wings out-stretched and beak open. Before their eyes adjusted to the darkness, a waiting sergeant on each side grasped each arm between the elbow and shoulder, jerking them to a halt. The sergeant on the left grabbed a blue cardboard ticket and thrust it into the soldier's hand. Then he shouted out the soldier's name, serial number, and the number on the blue ticket to an officer standing behind him, who in turn recited the same to another officer sitting at a table. When that officer nodded, the soldier's arms were released and he was shoved forward.

And he was given two identification tags, round aluminum, each the size of a silver dollar. James Lewis Green and Virginia

and a serial number (07141789): these three items had been
stamped on the disc. The rest of the disc was blank. There was
a hole in it and a chain to wear around his neck. He was told to
never take it off.

The number on the blue piece of cardboard was 1404.
Unknown to him, he had been assigned to HMS *Charybdis*.

The floor of the building was black-painted random oak
plank, the paint so worn and scuffed that the grain in the
wood was clear, almost raised. There was no furniture, though
what appeared to be a collapsed bandstand had been shoved
into a corner. Whitewashed numbers were painted around a
small circle in the middle of the floor, with an arrow pointed
outward from the integers. On each side of the number was a
straight line, radiating to an interior wall, together with its
companion sweeping out more area with their forward
progressions. Now corporals were screaming at the men,
telling them to approach the circle, look at the first two
numbers on their blue card, find those numbers on the floor,
and follow the arrows directly to the inside wall of the
building.

The roof of the Armory rested on pillars parallel to and
fifteen yards within the inside walls. Behind these pillars and
against these walls the men were directed to sit. The blue-card
numbers bore no relation to your squad, platoon, or company.
Buddy Green sat down within the widening radials defining
location fourteen. He had never seen the three soldiers already
there. But the air was cool, compared to that outside, and
relative darkness within the building hid its height. Almost
like a cave. It was with that thought, that geological
comparison, that there arose within Buddy Green the
primordium, the first hint by a thin and tentative tremolo, of
the relentless treadmill to which he had become bound.

The sun through the narrow windows fashioned a fanswise
coronet of light upon the Armory floor, with musical motes of
dust dancing in the seeping rays. As the day advanced, the
light narrowed to brushstroke sun prints, to hard-edged
shadow, to—and then past—the portcullis of night.

There was no food, a major explained, because the men were to have been loaded at 5 p.m. now four hours past. But that embarcation had been "overtaken by events." The men were to sleep on the floor, making sure they retained their blue piece of cardboard.

Buddy Green's portion of the radial had filled up, with soldiers whose blue cardboard numbered 1400 to 1460. There was still no soldier that he knew. Buddy Green, with fifty-nine other soldiers, placed his head upon his duffel bag and prepared to sleep. He placed his duffel next to the wall, and in a gap between the wainscot and the concrete he found a dried sprig of pine. Evergreen sprays had decorated the 1913 exhibition of modern art held at this Armory, where Cezanne's *Femme au Chapelet* and Van Gogh's *Montagnes a Saint Remy* had been displayed. Buddy Green would not have recognized those names. He crushed the sprig and held it to his face, inhaling Christmas.

....

The next morning they arose, as directed, at 5 a.m. No breakfast. In groups of 200–three groups—they were marched, if that is the word, in tattered columns, by disgusted Marine sergeants—disgusted by the marching—out of the Armory. These Army replacements had not learned how to march.

Through various streets and avenues, across a towering bridge, into the Brooklyn Navy Yard they trudged. Buddy was in the second group. There, at dockside awaited the HMS *Charybdis*.

The *Charybdis* had been built in 1905 by Workman-Clark, Ltd, in Dublin, for a Scots shipping firm, McDonald & Son, in Newcastle. The owners had drawn the specifications for the builder. It was 400 feet long, drew only forty feet of water, and was to be used to carry coal in bunkers from Newcastle on the Tyne down the coast, up the Thames, to London. Its engines—oil fired semi-turbines—were located below the now third steerage.

The coal had been mined north of Newcastle, from various mines, and shipped by rail to dockside there. From London, usually carrying limited cargoes of whisky, spices, salt, pepper in secure barrels; finished machine components in wooden crates, all as ballast, to Newcastle on the return trip. The ship had then no other economic use. Top speed was ten knots. Its keel was too shallow for stability on open ocean travel. The crew were and remained all Scots—at the owner's strict directive.

On January 4, 1918, the *Charybdis* was requisitioned by His Majesty's Government for use as a troop transport. The bunkers had been ripped out and bunks for men, three layers deep, were installed on three hastily constructed levels, winding stairs between and upwards to the main deck. A forward deck gun had been added, with the Scots crew instructed as to how to use it. Of course, they never practiced —bringing up ammunition, loading, aiming, firing—after the initial schooling, rendering the weapon essentially worthless.

There was only twenty-four inches of space between bunks. One had to slither in and out, like a snake from under a rock. Thin horsehair mattresses. No sheets, no blankets. Your backpack, your pillow. No space was designated for eating. You ate standing beside your bunk.

Beneath the bridge, that level contained cooking facilities, storage for food supplies, a toilet, a sick bay, various sized cabins, one for the ship's crew, one for the Navy seamen, one for the Navy lieutenant and the Navy ensign and an ancient Navy doctor, one for the Scots engineering officer and the Captain's executive officer, and one for the Captain. Therein was a small table, where the Captain and one invited guest could be served.

Water was supplied for the lower four decks—three steerage, and the engine compartment—by water butts, five per deck, much larger than those used at camp Lee. It was always somehow stale, tasting faintly of oil. There was no way to add bathrooms to discharge their contents in the sea; wooden seats over metal barrels were installed. There was room, in theory, for 600 soldiers, but they could only cram in 420–140 per deck. Ballast, adjacent to the engine compartment, was now crates of rifles—1903 Springfields and ammunition, 75-millimeter artillery shells. Thus the waterline became lowered.

Food and water was supplied from the first deck to the second, third, and fourth by large steel-cabled dumbwaiters— food, mess tins, water butts, metal barrels, up and down.

Buddy's contingent climbed up a wooden ramp. The American Navy ensign counted them and checked Buddy's blue card (1404) against a typewritten list. Buddy wondered why they did not use his new identification serial number. Of course, the paperwork had not caught up.

He was assigned to third deck steerage, below the water line, just above the engines. A lieutenant, the ensign, a grizzled old doctor, and eight seaman, were onboard—all regular Navy.

....

After loading the soldiers, the *Charybdis* remained moored for one night in Brooklyn harbor. Ballast and supplies, the Navy regulars, had been onboard for two days. At 6 a.m., after being turned by a tug and being escorted by a pilot boat, the ship entered the open ocean. It was met by a U.S Coast Guard cutter, which led the ship northward. Off Boston, a second troopship joined and off Newport another.

All three moored that night in Halifax Harbor, Nova Scotia. The next morning four cargo ships joined, and the little fleet headed east, slowly, through banks of fog, resonant horns orderly sounding the warning. They were to be escorted by a U.S. Navy destroyer for 150 miles—the distance that warship's fuel permitted for the trip out and back. They would be met by a British destroyer 150 miles from their destination. Between was the "Death Zone," beyond escort but not beyond the range of German submarines.

The ship's screws carved foaming hollows in the exterior of the sea. The muted twirling of the ship's wake; the constant running sound of the water sliding across the ship's sides; particles of sunlight projected in chert flakes, in ordered angles dictated off the surface of the sea by the progression of the sun: these were seldom to be seen or heard by any soldier.

Third steerage was a steel-encompassed hell. The heat was an oppressive presence, continuously rising from the engine room just below. And that air filled with coal dust, released from repose by the rolling of the ship. There was no silence. The dull sound of the engines likewise rose in muffled vibrations, not unlike continuous earth tremors, trembling the floor. Soon after leaving Brooklyn sea sickness arose. The *Charybdis* rolled back and forth, wobbling, a too short keel unable to provide stability in the open ocean.

Vomit from men unable to timely reach the latrine barrels accumulated on the steel decking, and urine and feces from those too long awaiting the same barrels, and small measures of tears from men crying in their bunks at night. A sloshing stench. The Navy seaman, who began the voyage checking on the soldiers, and counting them each morning and evening, retreated from their duty, presumably forging their daily reports to the officers.

Early on, some soldiers, with a permission slip signed by a Navy seaman, struggled up the winding stairs to the sick bay. The old Navy doctor never found one sick. And they struggled down the stairs. Soon the soldiers learned it was futile to report to the sick bay.

The food: weak watered tea; cider, turned vinegar and sour; tinned "bully beef" covered by congealed fat; canned mashed peas; Dr. Wills's "tatties" mixed with unknown "neeps;" something called "Maconohie" (pressed mystery meat and carrots); moldy bread suffused with weevils, or "skippers," as Buddy's siblings called them at home. Such food only served for supper. There was no lunch. For breakfast, thin oatmeal, with a pinch of brown sugar. Little food was actually eaten. Buddy had never before eaten oats. Like Doctor Samuel Johnson, Buddy thought oats were only for horses and Scots. Dr. Wills had once mentioned oats, in passing, not as a request to eat. Well, the *Charybdis* was crewed by Scots. The ship's crew and the Navy Regulars of course, had fresh food, on their reserved deck.

The only relief from this rolling hell came as groups of fifty, every other day, on shaking legs, slowly twirled up the winding stairs upwards to the open deck. This trip was the tiny cherished visit to the joy of the open air and sky.

But it was for purposes:

A U.S. Navy seaman led ordered physical exercises, to be performed in unison. They never were. The soldiers were so exhausted by lack of sleep, so drained by dehydration, that, over the course of the voyage they shortened, the Navy seaman recognizing they caused more harm than good. The exercises ended seven days into the voyage.

And also, lifeboat and life preserver drill— in case of abandoning ship—instructed by a bellowing Scots crewman. Sometimes Buddy had to translate the brogue to surrounding bewildered soldiers. But the soldiers soon recognized there were not enough lifeboats, or life preservers, far too few to accommodate them, knowing that upon abandoning ship, all would be used, first, by the crew of the *Charybdis* and the U.S. Navy regulars. Again, a worthless endeavor, but never shortened, as had been the physical fitness drills.

On the open deck they were also offered a salt water bath, in platforms fearfully hanging over the sea from the sides of the ship. No soap or towels were included in that offer, and the sea water and air were cold in these latitudes. About ten percent of the soldiers accepted the offer.

They regretted it. And their conclusion spread among the remaining.

Finally, though, a welcomed enterprise: submarine watch though the "Death Zone," blissful hours rotating every other day, in four-hour shifts throughout the day and night, with telescopes for every tenth man of the group of fifty. They were never told exactly what to look for, except for an extended piece of traveling steel above the water, or for water churning in a straight line for unknown reasons, or for similar bubbles arising on the surface of the water aiming towards the ship. They never saw any such motion. Sometimes at night, lightning, a jagged flash of phosphorus, illuminated the sea.

As promised, 150 miles out, a British destroyer reached

them, and headed the tiny fleet, and led them to their assigned port. That port was Brest, France.

6

They had been on the troopship for five days before Buddy saw land. Not land exactly, for there was a sandbar outside the harbour, and they had to wait for two days for the tide to sufficiently rise to make a landing. With the tide, the ship gently followed the thrusts and reverses of the current. And when the wind shifted, the brine-scented sea breeze was replaced with a different accent on the wind—the smell of baking bread.

When the wind died, the sea was still as the water atop a rain barrel at Cherry Hill. He was told the town was called Brest. He remembered Dr. Wills had landed here.

He also remembered a Bible verse, Ecclesiasticus 1:2 ("The sand of the sea and the raindrops, and the days of eternity, who can measure them?")

His group of fifty was ordered to await on the deck. Twenty-five minutes later, his group shuffled down the improvised wooden departure ramp—rails bending under their steps, giving a false spring to each staggered, reluctant journey downward. It terminated on a large stone quay—Buddy recognized the stone as granite—fine-grained ancient block, precisely fitted.

They were directed by shouting sergeants to a street heading inland. The street was cobblestoned, and their hobnailed boots clattered on the same.

There were groups of people—women, children, broken old men—standing beside the road all dressed in black. Silent.

One soldier said to Buddy:

They cheered us in New York when we boarded that damned ship before we got on it. What's wrong with these people? We are here to help France win this war. Why don't they at least do something to recognize us, clap or something?

It was July 14, 1918, which Buddy knew was Bastille Day, the French 4th of July. Should not they be celebrating? He did not know that those women and children had learned four days before that over 11,000 men of Brest had now been killed in action. And he did not understand that these mourners in black knew more, much more, of war than did he.

They marched, raggedly, about three miles inland, where there were scores of numbered conical tents located in a vast muddy field. It was a holding area for newly arrived soldiers, they were told. They were lined up, and an old white-haired major assigned each man to a tent as they walked by. Buddy was assigned to tent 183, along with nine others. No directions were offered, because that would slow the line. It took him almost twenty minutes to find tent 183, as no one arriving knew where or how the tents were arranged. They were not in numerical order, or in any perceivable order. When he arrived at 183, he did not know any of the others there, or any of the other soldiers who drifted in later. None were Virginians.

No rations were issued to them that day. And those later were poor. Beef stew in tins to eat after heating, but there were no fires allowed to heat them. There was pretty good bread, unlike anything Buddy had tasted, French bread. There were wells in the camp, but they were told not to use them. Too much filth had seeped in. Barrels outside, too far away for ease, contained water, sour from old wine. The camp was temporary, it was said. You can endure it. It's just for a while.

....

On YMCA stationery labeled "On Active Service with the American Expeditionary Force":

September 19, 1918

Dear Mother and All

I don't know how much of this will get through to you. The officers read and "censor" the mail so the Germans can't read what we write that might give them ideas about what we are doing. I arrived here safely at a place called….France. It was the same place where Dr. Wills landed many years ago. I spent…. days on the troopship and the conditions were…It is pretty cold here. I hope you all had a good crop of corn. Did you finish harvesting? Did you commence to fill the barn yet? The rumor here is that a bunch of us are to be sent somewhere in…of France where a…..is planned. You all take good care of yourselves. I have to stop writing now so I can get this to the sergeant who picks up the mail and takes it somewhere to be sent on. I hope it gets to you. Please write to me. The address is to me at A.P.O E.F..No……., …….,France. I remain as always your loving son and brother.

Buddy

……………

Ten days later, a sergeant entered tent 183 and told the ten men to report to the assignment center, a large cinder block building set up on the only high ground visible from the tents. Broken wooden stairs led upward to an open room. There sat, in a large bedraggled soft chair, with a bottle of rye and wine-glass on a table, a fat bald major.

Green, he bellowed.

Buddy stepped forward and, at attention, he saluted. He was directed to show his identification tag.

The Major checked it off a typewritten list.

Have you got any money with you?

Yes sir, I have two silver dollars. (Though Buddy had eleven back in his tent, dug into the ground underneath his cot.)

Well, I'm going to do you a favor. These frog money exchangers will cheat you. They will only give you thirty francs for each. I'll give you thirty-five. Let me see those American dollars.

Buddy handed over the silver dollars, given to him by his mother when he left for training camp. He received ninety francs. Later, he would learn what each silver dollar was really worth in francs, much more, a lot more most times, at towns inland, and even in Paris. He did not know then how the Major had cheated him.

The major continued:

Here is a military train ticket. It's good anytime, on any train, military or not. It's to Sivry-La-Perche, down near Verdun. Can only use it once. The train ticket is good from anywhere in France. It's one way. They're sending all you replacements down there. We call it Silver Peach. You have to be there on August twentieth. Wait a minute. There must be a screw up. The others are supposed to be there on August twentieth. Some typing error, I guess. Some idiot put nine instead of eight and eleven instead of twenty. Do you have some pull somewhere?

Buddy said:

No sir.

The major:

You are one lucky bastard. You have almost a week or so to fuck off. Go to Paris. There's plenty of good wine and food there—and lots of fuckable war widows. I tell you what: since we transacted for those silver dollars, I'm going to do you a favor. I'll give you a military railroad pass from Brest to Paris, one way. You'll have four days there. I wish I could go too, but no leave for me for a month. Remember, you are to report to the replacement and assignment office down there at Silver Peach on September fourteenth. Here is a second pass. You can use this pass from Paris to the Peach. Don't get tied up in Paris. Down at the Peach they will tell you where to go. Here are your written orders. Do not lose them.

Buddy put the papers in his tunic pocket.

Get out of here. There are a whole bunch of other fools in line.

All of the others in tent 183 were to arrive in Sivry-La-Perche on August 20. Buddy, remembering Dr. Wills's trip to Paris, decided to go there if only for four days.

....

He remembered what the professor had told him years ago, when he was fourteen:

Laddie, have you ever seen a sword, a real one?

Yes, my mother keeps one she thought was hidden in the

barn. But I have seen it, I told her. She said it was a Yankee sword. He got shot—she never said by whom—right here—while he was stealing. He was pushing a thin rod into the ground to find anything buried and had found some silverware—old from England. The Yankees had already stolen anything that moved—chickens, cows—and smoked hams. And had burned down the outbuildings several weeks before. She told me never to touch the sword or mention it to anyone.

Well, laddie, I shall tell you a story. I was about fourteen or so, your age, and I was walking up in the Braid Hills—you know, the hills near Edinburgh— trying to get inspired to be another Bobbie Burns—dinna work. Anyway, I saw a big tree down, roots a-dangling, and them still wet. Must have just fallen down, old age, I speculated. But on the side of the tree was an opening—looked ancient—probably a lightning strike—about what would have been head high when the tree was upright. I saw a glint. And I found a sword. Only the tip was rusted, at the bottom of the split—rainwater, I guess. The rest was as shiny as a new English shilling. Its handle had a sort of twisted metal wound around it. I showed my Da, and he told me to put it away for another day. I wrapped it in a sheepskin. I took it out sometimes and put the oil on it.

Two years later, I was off to the University. Now we weren't mint but we weren't skint either. But Da said, 'I paid for the first year, but you pay for the next; see what your sword is worth.' Da was a good man to me, from the time I was a wee lad, in the upbringing; but he could squeeze blood out of a five-pence coin. 'Waste not want not' was his motto. And so was 'Neither a borrower nor a lender be.' Good advice, and I have followed it. Not the first too well.

So I took the sword to old man Andrew McNarry's shop. He sold old things—coins, silverware, dirks, china, ball and powder pistols, and swords—most everything that was old. But people knew he was honest and true. Wasn't a cheater. And guess what? That sword was French, made about 1725, he said, and probably came over with Bonnie Prince Charlie. Some soldier of the Prince hid it, he said, to try and not be seen as what he was—so the English wouldn't kill him. McNarry looked amazed. He said he had never seen one—and he had seen about thirty of them—never one so shiny. He gave me

100 English pounds for it. Probably sold it for more, to some minted gentleman—if you can be minted and a gentleman too. But he was fair to me. Da only made about 400 English pounds a year. The fee for the University of Edinburgh was only fifteen English pounds a year, and I could live at home—Da let me. I was minted a little, for a youngster. I was eighteen then, and when the summer came I took twenty-five pounds and shipped to France—Dutch ship— see the world. Da said don't come back with the pox. Again, good advice.

Go to Paris, if you ever get to France. Landed at a town called Brest. Steam train—not nearly as good as ours, or as fast—to Paris. They had a revolution there in 1789, on July fourteenth. That's their Fourth of July, like you Americans celebrate. A bunch chopped off the king's head, and then his wife's, and lots of others. Then another bunch cut off the heads of the first killers. You can go to the place where they did it. Called the Place de Concorde now. Bloody Frogs.

Old Boney arrived and stopped all that. But we got him at Waterloo in 1815. English claimed they won it. But some Germans helped. And we did too—it was us Scots who probably won the battle, but you won't read about that in England.

The English took Old Boney off to an island way down in the south Atlantic, where he died. But the French dug him up and re-buried him in Paris, in a place called the "Invalides." You can see him there in a big marble tomb. There's a big church there called Notre Dame. Big beautiful windows, up high, with roses. Biggest kirk you'll ever see. But it's Papist. Don't let them priests talk to you. They'll try to make you a Papist.

The buildings are tall in Paris and there are hills on each side of the river, the Seine, that runs through the place, and islands in the river where the Courts are. I was told that the city was full of twisty dirty streets, and in the 1860s they knocked down all the old buildings and made the streets very wide. You would be hard pressed to hurl a stone across them. Streets as wide as the buildings are tall. They did it so cannons could shoot straight down them, in case the people got fractious again.

And there's a large art gallery, called the Louvre, where there are lots of paintings, and sculptures, and old cups and such treasures. And the paintings are not like the ones around here—like in the

Culpeper courthouse—where there are just bearded old men. They don't have any Scotch whiskey in Paris, not a dram, damn them, just rotten-tasting wine. But some good foods, especially bread.

Well, enough said.

Except, Bonnie Prince Charlie. He was English, son of a King the English got rid of. Bonnie Prince was exiled in France, along with his father. He was a Papist. He landed in Scotland, up north of Edinburgh, in 1745, and said he was going to get his crown back by beating the English. And a lot of folks agreed to help him, mainly Highlander Scots, who hated the English. We Scots in the South did not join—we were cannie. Because over at Culloden Moor, the English army crushed him, and he ran away and hid for a while and got back to France. Nobody knew how. Maybe my sword was his, but I doubt it.

....

The train to Paris was supposed to be direct. But it became a local, often pulling into sidings, its engine panting, sometimes for an hour, to allow other trains, deemed more important by the French government or military, to command preference.

His military pass limited him to third class. During such a demanded siding pause, he wandered forward, marveling at the array of French citizens, mainly old, poorly dressed, universally appearing despondent, angry or asleep, with assorted bags or suitcases, at their feet, also regulated to third class. Buddy was in uniform.

In the fourth car he entered, he saw a U.S. Marine first lieutenant, smartly clothed in dress blues, with an empty seat beside him. He was surprised that an officer was seated in a third-class car, later learning only colonels, and bird colonels at that, were allotted more genteel train accommodations.

He inquired if he could join the lieutenant.

Sit down, soldier, you are the only other American I have seen on this rickety train.

They exchanged names and histories, and to his joy he learned the lieutenant was Albert Francois Duncan, from Lexington, Virginia, at the lower end of the Valley over the mountains. He had finally chanced upon a fellow Virginian.

The lieutenant had graduated in 1916 from the Virginia Military Academy, in his hometown, and had chosen to join the Marines, rather than the Army.

The lieutenant's grandparents, Coke and Ayliffe Duncan, were themselves originally from Scotland. Remembering the tales of the old French connection to Scotland, during the troubled times with the English, they had emigrated in 1855, settling in La Rochelle, a town on the French coast. Behind were left some never-mentioned problems.

There the lieutenant's father, named Wallace, was born. He married a French girl named Marie DuBois and trained as an engraver, of paper, on copper sheeting, or anything receptive to his skill. Because of a lingering economic depression in France, his parents, recognizing the many opportunities offered to do so in their commercial shipping town, and repeatedly hearing of the booming prosperity in the United States, after much consideration, left for that country, in 1890, on a Dutch freighter, the *Zeelandia*.

Wallace carried with him French currency, all of gold, saved from proceeds of the sale of all their furniture and furnishings. But Wallace retained his engraving tools—a scarper, for carving out metal; a split-stick, for fluid lines; and an engraver, for cutting lines that swelled or shrunk, depending on the angle used. The set, enclosed in pockets of a heavy canvas bag, had been made in 1880, by Euracier, fine tool makers in Saint-Brice-sous-Foret, France.

Wallace had retained some memory of his father's English, and, in the months before their departure, was tutored in the same, in the basement of an Anglian church.

His parents' ship arrived in Norfolk, Virginia. A French-born storekeeper, on a weekly basis, graciously read to his father advertisements in the *News-Ledger* for appropriate work, commensurate with his training. A small publisher and newspaper owner, in Lexington, Virginia, named Angus McNair, offered employment; and he and Marie, encouraged by that name, immediately left by train for that town.

McNair, learning Wallace's ancestors, noting his Christian

name, and sternly but fairly testing his skill as an engraver, quickly hired him, in 1891. There Wallace remained employed for all his remaining years—and, with McNair's permission, part time engraving items at William Sale's jewelry store.

Albert was born in Lexington in 1892, and thus was an American citizen. Albert had grown tall, graduated from Rockbridge County High School, and was bilingual, French being spoken by his parents at home. That language asset was noted when he appeared before the faculty admissions committee at VMI. French was then the language of diplomacy, and he was admitted. Later, that language facility was noted by the Marines, and he was assigned to a company that acted as security for the U.S. Embassy in Paris. They had other duties.

He told Buddy:

When we get to Paris, you must register with the American Embassy. We provide aid for our soldiers—a pamphlet with various explanations, even a little French money—and will find you an approved place to stay during your leave. I'll take you there when we reach Paris. I have to report in.

Soon thereafter the train arrived at the Gare d'Orsay, on the eastern side of the city.

7

Buddy and Lieutenant Duncan arrived at the Gare d' Orsay. Buddy had never seen a building so large—steel and glass, soaring, with eight parallel tracks, all with engines steaming and idling, people swarming, shouting in multiple languages, laden carts of baggage, coming and going along the landings beside the trains.

The lieutenant said he would lead him to the Embassy, which was on the Rue de Chaillot Prints.

As they walked along, Buddy was astonished at the size and magnificence of Paris—avenues more spacious, wider and buildings, hundreds, taller than he had ever seen. Statues, manicured parks, restaurants with awnings, shops each offering single, or only several, items for sale. Dr. Wills's description had not done this city justice.

Hundreds of soldiers in many colored uniforms he had never seen, their counties of origin announced by the lieutenant as they passed, subtly pointing: England, Belgium, some French Black African place, Scotland, South Africa, Australia, New Zealand, French Algeria, French Morocco—if you work at the Embassy, they recognize them all. But not all of them fight hard. At least not like Marines. They need them all, though, because so many Brits and Scots, and especially French, have been casualties, out of the war—wounded, or dead. A lot of them really don't do much, driving trucks, caring for animals, unloading and loading supplies, cooking, carrying wounded—that kind of work, not combat.

Sidewalks streaming with men and women, smartly dressed in what he assumed was French high fashion—men's hats of strange shapes, shoes with white short leggings of unknown purpose, numerous canes, little dogs with fancy leashes, some with colored stones imbedded, women's hats a yard wide with fake flowers and real feathers. No one, even on Rules Day, in Culpeper would be so ostentatious, so gaudy, so immodest. It was as if they did not know there was a war, or didn't care. They generated no respect in Buddy's mind.

When they reached the Embassy, pausing on the broad front steps, the lieutenant said:

I'll take you in, show you where to go, maybe the colonel will be in and perhaps you could even meet him. He cares about all Marines. He greets as many as his duties permit. But he usually has to escort the damn politicians when they arrive to tell us what to do, no matter how senseless. They understand nothing, I think. The colonel fought in the Philippines, and he knows what war is all about. If he's had a drink or two he will sometimes mention incidents there, but not often.

The front door was of tall massive double chestnut halves; it was guarded on each side by a massive Marine in dress uniform, with .45 Colts in polished holsters, shoes shining even brighter. They each saluted, the Lieutenant returning the gesture, and opened each of the bisected entrances. Buddy entered, following the lieutenant. He forgot to salute the Marines, and hoped he hadn't offended them.

....

1911 was a year of severe drought in parts of France. The Loire river was at its lowest level in 200 years, especially at Nevers. The lead pipe, containing our lead, was revealed. The city authorities asserted ownership, and that claim was not challenged. The lead's existence became the subject of several regional newspapers. One story was repeated in *Paris-Match*. An employee of Marcel Bleustein-Blanchet, French scrap metal dealers in Cambrai, on the Belgium border, read that newspaper and passed on the information to his employers. A firm representative left immediately for the town on the Loire. There, after two days of tense negotiations, he purchased the lead for 1,500 francs. At his direction, a local blacksmith cut the pipe into rectangular bars. One bar contained our lead. The bars were taken by cart to the railroad station, and shipped to the scrap dealer in Cambrai.

....

When Buddy and Lieutenant Duncan entered the Embassy, it turned out the colonel was in his office; after inquiring of a Marine sitting outside his door, they were permitted to enter. The lieutenant saluted, and Buddy, thankfully, remembered to do likewise. On the colonel's desk was a nameplate: "Lt. Colonel B.W. Gayle," as the silver oak leaf on his shoulder epaulettes indicated.

He said:

Let me see your identification disk, son, and your orders.

Buddy produced them, and the Colonel made a note on a small paper pad.

In the office to the right outside is a clerk. He will attend to your needs. Good Day.

Saying, "Yes, Sir" and saluting again, Buddy left as he had been directed, and slowly shut the door.

The Lieutenant had stayed behind. Buddy never saw him again. The clerk turned out to be a Marine lance corporal, wearing glasses. Behind his desk were four metal filing cases, and a safe. He too requested Buddy's identification disc and orders. Opening a file cabinet he pulled out a folder filled with forms.

The first was a printed map of the right bank of Paris, with red lines all radiating from the Embassy, designating, along the most direct routes, places to see, each named—Invalides, Place de la Concorde, Notre Dame, Louvre, Sacred Coeur, Tuileries Gardens.

The next form showed the size, color, and value of French coins: centime, two franc, five franc, ten franc, and twenty franc.

Next was an English/French translation guide:

I am an American soldier; I do not speak French, do you speak English?; Please; Thank you; Take me to the United States Embassy; I am sick.

Also there were the French names for various foods: water, milk, butter, bread, beans, potatoes, tobacco, matches, chicken, beef, jam, coffee.

The corporal said:

Just point out the words to a Frenchman, and he will know what you mean. Buddy wondered what soldiers who could not read would do.

From a drawer in the bottom of his desk, the corporal pulled up a sheet of paper, reviewing it:

We provide a place to stay for soldiers on short term leave, as are you. We pay for it, but you must tip, pay a gratuity, to the person who runs it, usually an old woman called a "concierge." Your place is ninety-eight Rue Motorglueil. It is down near the big market, Les Halles. Watch, I'm going to draw directions from here to there on the map. Now, if you have any American, we can exchange it for French money.

Buddy brought out two silver dollars.

You got more money than most guys.

He turned around, spun the dial, backwards and forwards, and opened the safe. He gave Buddy 110 francs for each. And Buddy then realized how cheated he had been by the drunken major in Brest.

Now, our regulations require we give you twenty francs, regardless of how much money you have, for emergency use only— emergency only.

He handed that sum over, and required Buddy to sign a receipt for the entire 240 francs, and sign on each form, including his identification number.

Private Butler, sitting there, will take you to the place you are to stay, and make sure you get in. He speaks much better French than I do. Oh, before you go, the colonel wants to see you. Just knock, and if he says, "Enter," go in.

In the manner instructed, Buddy went in, again

remembering to salute. The colonel did not return it.

Now, soldier, you're lucky I'm here and have got the time. I am going to give you some good advice, and you better damn sight follow it. First, don't go with a whore. They're all diseased, and you know, they told you in training, what that will do to you. And if you come back here whining because you got the clap, we will court-martial you. Second, if you aren't on that train to Silver Peach, at the time and day your orders require, we will find you, and we will shoot you. Get out of here. Good Luck, and God bless.

Backing away, forgetting to salute, Buddy quietly and gently opened and then closed the door behind him. By then, it was almost 6 p.m.

Lieutenant Duncan, then a Captain, died in 1924, as part of the U.S. Marine contingent during the occupation of Haiti. He died in a hospital tent, of dysentery, feverish but shaking with chills, enswathed with feces, aswarm with flies.

....

With numerous windings, Private Butler led Buddy to 98 Rue Motoglueil from the Embassy, showing him the tracery on the map. He stopped and knocked on a door. Surprising Buddy, only the top half opened. There was an old woman, in a sagging gray dress, with a scarf on her head, and a yellow apron. He noticed an old French telephone on a small table behind her. She smiled, recognizing Private Butler's uniform, and they engaged in what seemed lengthy conversation. The private handed her a typewritten piece of paper, in French. She slowly read it, and nodded. Apparently the private required her to read it back to him. He handed her an amount of money, an amount Buddy could not see.

He told Buddy:

Your room is paid for the four nights you will be here. She will show you the room. It won't be much, but it's clean—we inspect before we add a place to our list. You may be sure it's better than where you are going. After she shows it to you, you must pay her five francs. Show me you know that coin. That's it. You must always knock on this door, whenever you leave or enter, and make sure the lady actually sees you. Remember that or there will be trouble. Be on that train to the Peach. Good luck!

Buddy did not know that the piece of paper instructed the woman to immediately call a given number at the Embassy if he did not return every night during his leave, or if he returned here after his ordered departure date, a date supplied on those instructions. This was the same as prior agreements, and harshly enforced. A bonus was offered for a prompt report.

The narrow room, on the third floor, reached by a winding staircase, contained a single bed without a sheet, a thin mattress, two blankets, a feather pillow, a small table, wooden hangers hanging from nails on the reverse of the door, a small bowl for water, and a china chamber pot. Water was available at a spout in the backyard, as was a privy. Buddy, as directed, handed her a five franc piece; without acknowledging its receipt, she silently placed it in a pocket of her apron. There was no window. But, anyway, it was already dark.

Exhausted from the train trip, and his time at the Embassy, Buddy lay down and slept, into the night

....

During his first night at 98 Rue Motorguiel, Buddy was awakened during the early mornings hours, fitfully, only momentarily, by the sounds of shouts, curses, lorries, carts, wagons, emanating from an adjacent cobbled roadway.

The next morning, after notifying the concierge, he stepped out into bright sunlight. Before him stood a building, larger than the Gare d'Orsay, with numbers of arched entrances, brick and iron construction, paint-encrusted rivets, skylights. Outside, scores of vendors, entreating their offerings to those passing on the connecting and converging roads. It was Les Halles, the market of Paris, the "belly of Paris."

Amazed at the sight, he walked into an entrance. He found an almost incomprehensible cornucopia of fruits, vegetables, and meats he could not always recognize, flowers, pots, pans, with each proprietor calling out. Carts laden, unladen, re-laden swarmed back and forth. Water dripping from stalls, ice melting. With a laugh, he noticed a skinned rabbit, for some reason with its ears and tail still attached. Here, each day over the next two, he bought fruit for lunch. Peaches, apples, and raspberries. It was like Rules Day at home, multiplied by thousands, and much too shrill, without dignity or graciousness.

....

One afternoon, following the line on his map, Buddy entered the Tuileries Gardens. There were winding gravel walks, with interspersed benches he noticed were marble, streaked with red, gray, black, green—he wondered what chemicals, what elements, what atoms, had so marked them. Gaslights on intricate iron constructs, awaiting evening. Fancy dressed women, with little children in tow, or in small carriages, old men smoking pipes, reading newspapers on benches, couples strolling.

He recognized trees of cherry, chestnut, dogwood, crepe myrtle, maples now red-leaved, as he remembered from the foothills of the Blue Ridge. Some trees, gnarled, others slender trunked and tall, some like, but then unlike, pines at home. Hedges shaped into animal forms, which he found unnatural and unnerving.

And flowers—acres of purple and white asters, daffodils and jonquils and tulips and roses—somehow surviving into this fall.

A field of purple-headed stalks, clustered like ripe wheat. Individuals would approach and grind several stalks together, then raise their hands to their noses. To learn why, Buddy did likewise. For the first time, he inhaled lavender.

....

Buddy ate breakfast and supper on his three days at a small unpretentious restaurant located up the Rue de Motorguiel from where he stayed. Its patrons, only men moderately dressed, noticed his uniform. Some somberly, some with a grimacing knowing slight smile acknowledged his presence. They recognized his uniform, apparently. None ever approached him or spoke to him. They always had glass tumblers of wine before them. He never saw a woman in the place.

It was named the Cafe de la Fleur. He had memorized "please" and "thank you."

Using his phrase pamphlet, he pointed to coffee, milk, bread, butter, jam. The apron-clothed, bearded owner nodded. Within minutes, he set down at Buddy's small table a chipped blue cup —"cafe au lait"—two crescent-shaped pieces of bread, butter, and a small jar of purple jam. Buddy recognized the drink as coffee with hot milk, the bread and jam almost the finest he had ever tasted. The jam, black currant, was new to him, though it somehow generated the thought of tart blackberries.

Two dinners, again from the phrase aid (chicken, beans, and potatoes; beef, onions, and potatoes, each with water), somehow tasted unlike those so composed at home, but deliciously different. And the wonderful bread.

After each meal he held out his hand full of French coins and let the owner choose. The owner always smiled as he did so. Buddy had seen the prices for his meals, on a grease thickened menu, or chalked on a wall behind the bar. He correlated those prices with those coins which the proprietor chose. Perhaps he had been cheated, but he did not think so. The owner was honest, he concluded. Though perhaps that honesty was compelled by his uniform and consequences that might follow if cheating was reported by a U. S. soldier, one who well knew the language and the value of the coins. Many Parisians had heard, or learned, that the U.S Marines, distinguished by their uniforms, forcefully protected American soldiers.

....

One morning, as Buddy was strolling along and consulting his map, he saw a building designated thereon, as the Louvre. He remembered Dr. Wills's advice. He should visit it, a magnificent collection of paintings and objects.

The building was immense, and had been sandbagged along the entire foundation. He climbed steps upward and entered, through half opened tall wooden doors. Just inside was a booth, occupied by a one-armed older man, the left sleeve of his tunic pinned to his shoulder, the tunic garnished by a single tarnished military metal. That tunic was horizon blue, the original color of the earliest "poilus," the French informal name for their infantrymen. A sign above the booth read Entree 5.F.

Buddy reached into his tunic pocket and removed some money. The old soldier shook his head, touched his tunic, pointed at Buddy's uniform, and waved him in.

Only the first floor was open; stairs to upper floors had been closed, barred by metal gates. The great preponderance of the collection had been moved, for safety's sake, to the Château de Chambord, an estate of 13,000 acres straddling the Loire River far to the southeast of Paris.

Buddy walked along, gazing at paintings, and paused to examine three. One rendered men and women, in elegant old finery, strolling along, in bright sunlight and spring flowering trees, alongside a large building. Buddy recognized that building as this very one. It was painted by a man named Antoine Blanchard.

The second, *Bend in the Road*, by a painter called Paul Cézanne, reminded him of the woods and rocks upstream from the spring at home.

The third brought tears to his eyes, forced memories. Painted by Jean-Francois Millet and dated 1865, it rendered a man sowing grain by hand in a plowed field, a horse drawn plow at work in the background. He desperately wished he was doing the same, behind Blackie, in a field at Cherry Hill. There now, not here, in this foreign land. He slowly collected himself, and continued onward, embittered.

Among collected objects—statues, bowls, embroidery, shaped metal forms—he stopped before a pure white stature. It had been partially broken, the left arm missing from a man wearing a Roman cloak, or toga, a pallium. Buddy knew that it was marble, and he knew how it was formed, all from Dr. Wills's lectures. But with no other minerals, generating colors other than white. White, perhaps that which, whatever chemical, also hued the white quartz at home.

Toward leaving the museum, passing other objects, he abruptly stopped. Before him on the cherry wood table sat a cup. He stared at it, walking around the table to scan it from all sides, an ardent attention. He recognized its composition as silver. The silver was not engraved, only slightly delicately broadened at its top edge. It was about fifteen inches in height, its circumference gently increasing from approximately three inches at its base to approximately six at its upper rim. A label described it as a "Coptic cup, circa 4th Century A.D." It further explained, in French and English, that Copts were a Christian sect, still in existence, located primarily in Egypt and countries further south in Africa. Buddy had never heard of them.

For some reason within, undeciphered, he thought he had never seen anything so beautiful made by the hands of man. And subconscious in his mind was, then too not recognized, a proposition: the essence of beauty was proportion and order.

He entered into the adjacent grand boulevard, after returning the old French soldier's feeble salute, and felt leisurely cheered.

....

Buddy was walking along the Seine on the left bank when he saw Notre Dame towering over the Île de la Cité. Dr. Wills had told him to visit. He crossed the Pont Neuf. He had never seen a building so large or tall. It was a Thursday, late morning. Entering, he was stunned by the windows. Enormous glass windows with circles containing items of all the colors of the rainbow. He remembered the single glass window at the Amissville Methodist church—barely two feet square with Jesus spreading his arms, and only three colors.

Here, a vast number of seats, but there were only a 100 or so people in attendance, spread out in small groups. After walking up to a big cross, they would touch their chests, four times, and then sit in a pew. He remembered some men back in Hut 183 who would do the same, same chest touching, after looking at a small cross held on a chain around their necks. Some form of Papist recognition, he gathered.

Some people were well dressed, some obviously poor, some French soldiers, mostly mutilated—many missing an arm or a leg or a face horribly scarred. He had heard enough French to recognize that language they spoke, but two men were talking in a different language, constantly waving their hands as they did so.

His Mother always told him:

Don't wave your hands when you talk. Virginians do not do that. Now, describe for me a winding staircase and don't dare use your hands!

Many more people were entering, but from behind curtains to a large stage, and setting up some sort of tripods and putting sheets of music upon them. The musicians. There were scores and scores of them, but there were no uniforms. They were dressed as if they had just come from home, wearing whatever clothes they might have had on. Many fiddles and large fiddles which were upright. He recognized them, and drums and flutes and trumpets. But he had never seen French horns, trombones, or clarinets. Orchestra was not within his vocabulary.

Then many apparently singers came in behind the band— almost a hundred, both men and women, likewise casually dressed. The choir at Amissville was only seven women. Buddy concluded correctly that this was a rehearsal.

The first sound he heard was a long drawn out note on an organ. The organ was out of sight; it must have been enormous. It's sound filled all the space. So different than Mrs. Thatcher's small organ in Amissville, which she pedaled with her feet. Hers was a mouse compared to this mighty roaring lion.

Buddy did not know it, of course, but this was a rehearsal of Donizetti's requiem.

He sat silent, entranced, for over an hour. The sound filled him. Each note distilled, rising from liquid to vapor, and condensing to liquid again. The music rose, fell, and rose again. Interspersed with a hundred voices, punctuated by single voices at times. The close, lovely, reasoning helix of the stringed instruments. He thought he could actually see the music in the sun-channeled air in the cathedral.

Something shifted, it seemed to him, in his mind. The music seemed to become living, filling him, attaching to his bones as well as to his mind. A simple beauty impressed forever upon his soul. A quest for eternity. And it is said if you can hear music with deep intensity, the music can hear you. Buddy left Notre Dame, blinking into the afternoon sun, in some kind of trance.

8

Precisely on time—6:30 a.m.—and the day named and location designated on his orders, Buddy arrived at the Gare de l'Est in Paris. Earlier, he had knocked on the top half of the door, and gestured he was leaving, to the scowling awakened concierge. He had learned "Bon jour." He ate a quick breakfast at the Cafe de la Fleur and shook hands with the owner, who appeared surprised at the gesture.

At the Gare was an enormous tattered sign, an arrow pointing to the left, proclaiming: "U.S. ARMY PERSONNEL." Following the direction, he entered the rear of a line of soldiers, of different ranks, but mainly privates, as was he. One by one, they approached a sort of large booth, where two Army military police were seated, a haggard looking major between. When he finally appeared before them, the major asked to be shown his identification disc and his orders. He checked his name off a thick stapled-together list and pointed to the left, saying go to that M.P., standing perhaps fifty yards away. Relays of M.P.s directed him around to the side of the Gare, where on one of six parallel tracks sat a train, thirty wooden box cars long.

Each car was labeled in black: "40 HOMMES/ 8 CHEVAUX". Forty men, eight horses. Each car was vented with narrow open horizontal slats. In no apparent order, M.P.s had placed groups of fifty soldiers in each car, starting from the first, number one, and working their way backwards. They checked no orders, but required each soldier to have a full canteen and ordered any soldier with less than a full canteen to fill the same from parked water carts. Buddy's was full and he was placed, though he did not know the number, in car sixteen.

On two parallel tracks, French officers were directing black soldiers filling open cars with crated supplies, mainly ammunition, artillery shells, French machine guns, American B.A.R.s (Browning Automatic Rifles) and some tents and coils of barbed wire. All working in frantic motion—lorry contents to railroad car, lorry contents to railroad car.

The double doors of the troop-laden railroad cars were left open. And, during the two hour wait to complete loading, a view down the sides of the cars would include scores of soldiers, pissing outward.

Buddy's car, as were others, had bunches of filthy straw and flattened dung on the floor. Those conditions seemed to lengthen the wait. At 10 a.m., the car doors were closed, and locked. The cars were briefly shaken as the locomotive attached, then began to move, first slowly, toward the southeast, toward the Silver Peach.

. . . .

The trip from Paris to the Silver Peach took fourteen hours. The train appeared to have no constant speed—uneven— faster, then slower, then faster again. The train would stop to take on water and coal for the boilers. Shabby signal cabins, even in day time illuminated by a diffuse cone of light, dictated progress. And each time the couplings between cars, like ascending and descending discordant notes, would clash down and up the line, with each stop and start. Buddy thought of an old horse, stopping and starting. Blackie would be old, if he ever got home.

The soldiers were impressed by the unusual foresight of the mandated filling of canteens, though they necessarily caused an addition to the stench of the floors. And passing through dusty villages, girls would wave, or sometimes just stare, at the line of cars. The men would hoot and holler at them, generating foul talk of what they would do, or claim they had done, with such girls.

At times in the blue distance were seen peaceful gentle water meadows traversed by freshet streams.

At one stop rations were thrown into the cars—hardtack, canned tomatoes and corned beef. The soldiers were reminded only to sip the water in their canteens. The train left a trail of discarded empty tin cans in its wake.

Passing a stone bridge, Buddy saw pigeons, gray as the granite on which they clustered, the specks on their breasts sparkling as did the mineral—green-white mica flakes—in the granite itself. He thought of Guinea hens at home. At home.

At night, occasional sparks from the locomotive stack would flow past the car, reminding Buddy of distant shooting stars he had seen over the Blue Ridge mountains, again, at home.

The Silver Peach was a mid-sized town, with one large rail yard. Its main function was to serve as a depot to export the grain, livestock, wine, timber, and other agricultural products of farms within 150 miles, to points west, as Marseilles, Bordeaux, or to points north as Paris, Lyon. It had six railroad tracks, sufficient for this function, and sufficient tracks, now almost exclusively used to transport troops and military supplies to the "Sacred Way," the road to Verdun and the upcoming Meuse-Argonne offensive.

In the train yard, Buddy's train unloaded. Unlike the loading, here M.P.s assembled the soldiers in ten columns of five, marching them on the concrete ways beside the tracks and outward two miles, where continued transportation became available. Lorries.

....

From the railroad station at the Silver Peach, trucks—some Fords, mainly Renaults—were driven by black men, from some French African regiment. They took him and many others, over a road also jammed with lorries carrying ammunition and other supplies, staggered over the torn road, with military police shouting and pointing—trying to make some order. A chain of vehicles. Broken down trucks were pushed off onto adjacent fields. There was no time to repair them, and no replacements for them. Men and supplies were added to those remaining. It took fifteen hours for a truck to leave the Silver Peach and reach the encampments of various divisions surrounding the city of Verdun.

....

Verdun, an old medium-sized city, had been wrecked, nearly demolished, by German artillery during the three years it had withstood a German siege. It was located on several low intermittent hills, connected through shallow valleys by paved roads, stone bridges, and a tram. It had once been beautiful.

Outside the town, where the American division camps were constructed, also arose narrow, more modest hills, on some of which were located chateaus, now abandoned, likewise destroyed, once owned by wealthy families. Few full trees remained here, most shell torn, gaunt as giblets. Further out of town, to the south, lay farmlands.

Buddy saw refugees fleeing west from what they knew was coming. Old men and women staggering along by the side of the road with belongings tied to their backs; people pushing baby carriages, or wheelbarrows, filled with clothes, pots and pans; some pulling a rope tied to a hog, a sheep; chickens and geese with legs tied, strung around a child's neck. Some cursing; some crying. They were all in gray or black, with occasional spots of color on scarves. They walked as if asleep.

....

He reported to the replacement/assignment building, directed by a sweating military policeman. A drunken sergeant sent him, after checking his name and serial number against a list, further down the road to a sign saying 32nd Division, with an arrow pointing to a tent in a field. He entered the tent.

A master sergeant, the name Willowitz on a tag on his tunic, simply said:

Name?

Buddy replied:

James Lewis Green

Show me your identification tag and orders.

After inspecting them, he turned over a number of typewritten pages, held together by a pin, his finger trawling down.

The sergeant said:

You're from Virginia?

Yes, sergeant.

Another damned Johnny Reb. Why do they keep sending us you Rebs? We are Michigan and Wisconsin boys. We kicked your ass during the revolt.

Buddy remained silent. He remembered: cavalry soldiers from Michigan had horsewhipped his father.

The sergeant barked:

127th Regiment, Company F. Headquarters are down the road in the farmhouse painted—Ha!—green.

....

Company F was commanded by a Captain Metternich, with seven lieutenants and 190 men. That was on paper. But actually, there were only six lieutenants and 148 men—sickness, losses, limited replacements.

A First lieutenant named Anderson met Buddy, and again he was checked off a typewritten list by a clerk wearing glasses. The lieutenant motioned for a sergeant who gave Buddy a steel helmet. He had never worn one before. He was given a gas mask with a case and shown how to wear it. He had never seen one before. He was given two canteens and a mess kit.

He was given what they called a K-Bar, a sort of Bowie knife, and a bayonet, and sheaths for attaching each to his belt. He was given a tin medical kit marked with a red cross. He was given an entrenching tool—a spade with a folding handle.

The lieutenant called out in French and an old gnarled bearded Frenchman entered. Buddy was told to give him his tunic. The man sewed the 32nd Division patch on the right shoulder of his tunic. The patch was green, with a red arrow pointing upwards, with a red stripe horizontally through the shaft.

He was also given a 1903 Springfield, and 20 5-round clips, with a bag to hold them. The sergeant noticed the red Sharpshooter badge, and pointed it out to the Lieutenant. He was assigned to tent 16 or 17, which combined, held 30 men, a platoon. The platoon to which he was assigned, the 3rd of Company F, with a young Second Lieutenant named Thomas McCullough commanding, along with his First sergeant, named Penzler, who actually had war experience. Each carried a 1911 Colt .45 pistol in addition to their Springfields.

Penzler was bald, his skull as smooth as polished marble; splayed, sloping, shoulders; short, squat, massive legs; an expansive birthmark, the color of an overripe plum, covering his tight left jawbone, remaining luminous through any razor's venture. He kept a two-shot Colt derringer in his right leggings. And he kept a small French canteen containing grain alcohol, stolen from the aid station, attached to his belt.

With a small pressing machine, a corporal stamped "Company F, 127th Regiment, 32nd Division" on his aluminum identity discs . Those discs were now full.

The platoon lived in the two large adjoining tents, 15 each, each tent worn and battered, spotted with bluish-grey patches, cut from the rain-capes of dead French officers, to thwart the rain and snow. Small Iron stoves, coal-fired when that commodity was available, were vented by tin chimneys. Pieces of broken finished wood, or portions of shattered trees, were collected by forage parties, to supplement coal. Large copper water carts were interspersed throughout the camp, seldom full.

Latrines, filled, buried, and re-dug in another location, were occasionally doused with lime.

Food, only breakfast—coffee and bread, sometimes butter and jam and dinner—usually bully beef and canned vegetables. —was offered in lines stretching and inching towards the mess tent, manned by sweating, cursing old sergeants, surly masters of the immense greasy cauldrons.

9

The Meuse-Argonne region of France stretched from the Argonne Forest of dense thick undergrowth on the West to rising chalk, limestone, and granite heights, and other minor types of rock, above and immediately behind the Meuse River on the East. Between was a broad valley, twenty miles wide, though one with occasional modest hills and streams. On the most prominent hill was the town of Montfaucon (Mount Falcon), named for ground supporting it: it rose on the dominating hill, 1,250 feet high, in a region itself 1,000 feet above sea level.

There were no even mid-sized towns in the valley. Rather, it was farmland, and retained wood lots, near the scattered villages. But the villages were old, constructed over centuries, with houses, walls, and outbuildings of fitted stone won from not-too-distant quarries, sturdy timber, and slate roofs. Roads south, toward the city of Verdun, were few and unpaved. Those paths between villages, even more primitive.

....

These chalk, limestone, sandstone, and granite cliffs to the East were part of the Ardennes mountain chain. It was on old chain. A level of limestone contained fossils estimated at 382 million years old.

This chain of mountains, as are all, were formed by plate tectonics. The surface of the earth rests on seven plates, floating, if you will, on the hot core of the earth. At times, over millions of years, the edges of these plates collide, slowly, inches per year. And when they do, one plate yields, being crumbled upwards, forming mountains, the layers of the former surfaces, sometimes remaining level, on keel, sometimes twisted or turned. And thus fossils from a sea floor, or limestone or granite, become peaks, awaiting the inevitable assault of eroding wind and rain, and their reduction.

Sometimes the collision of plates forces one plate down, beneath the other, generating thousands of volcanoes, as the earth's molten core arises—with constituents of heavier elements, gold, iron, lead included—and solidifies, again as mountains. All the elements were also included in this igneous extrusion—some became granite—quartz, feldspar, alumina, magnesium—granite—as they solidified.

All collisions can, and do, by the generated pressure and heat, cause to melt original rock, changing one form of rock into another, melting and rearranging, taking away or adding to, the atoms of the original. But those atoms, in any change, always lock together, connect, in an orderly, never altering, manner.

. . . .

From Montfaucon, the Germans had excellent observation of 80% of the entire battlefield. The first German line of defense was moderately defended and designed for observation and to slow any attack. Their second line ran through Montfaucon, east and west. It had been stoutly constructed. It was the main bulwark of the German defense, and the controlling headquarters of the German Army in the region. The third German line was thinly defended, used primarily for logistics and the soldiers who served them.

To the natural obstacles of the Meuse-Argonne the Germans had added dugouts, trenches, concrete emplacements, hidden machine gun pits with interlocking fields of fire, miles of barbed wire, and concealed artillery positions. The majority of these constructs were in the second, but a substantial number were in the first line. The Germans had occupied the valley for almost four years and continually improved these defenses.

....

The 32nd had only about 70% veterans, having fought in battles over the preceding year and a half. 30% were gone— dead, wounded, sick, missing in action.

For two weeks, the new replacements trained: how to dig a foxhole, and keep it from falling in when it rained; how to try to escape machine gun fire if trapped in an ambush; how to distinguish the sound of German artillery in the air from friendly artillery; what the colors of different smoke grenades meant; what each number of whistle blasts meant; how to make a tourniquet from the strips of cloth in their medical kit; how to make a stretcher from saplings and belts. They were cautioned to drink no water, even from wells, as the Germans poisoned them with dead animals, or from streams, all polluted by capricious chemicals or soldiers' waste, only water from their canteen. And they spent plenty of time at a firing range.

....

Lieutenant Steiger was a thoughtful officer. He was tall, sandy haired, and wore thick glasses. Twice he would lead the platoon in excursions within 5,000 yards behind the front lines, over ground recently taken from the Germans, to show them what they must traverse when called into action. The ground was horrific. There were shell craters, some still smoking, dead bodies unidentifiable as American or German because so nearly destroyed and burnt, collapsed trenches, amazing amounts of discarded equipment—helmets, broken rifles, filthy bloody bandages, rifle stripper clips, broken carts, collapsed stretchers, backpacks, mangled boots, discarded rations.

But what struck, and slowed one, was mud. Different colors —some black, some yellow, some grayish, some lead colored. There seemed to be no truly solid soil. Puddles of water, of indecipherable depth, throughout every track forward.

Old roads, poorly repaired, over and over, by exhausted Army engineers. Repairs were never complete because the

German artillery, sometimes by barrage, sometimes just harassing fire, continuously shelled the roads, recognizing it totally disrupted supply to the front, and the removal of the wounded to the rear. A disjointed grid work of anarchy.

Once, when the lieutenant took his platoon out, Buddy, standing on a slight rise, saw within a narrow, shallow valley below, a tattered ovoid cluster of broad, somber and blackened tree stumps. They formed an island in the war -abandoned fields, those fields now churned by artillery fire into a fetid, foul domain of scrupulous sodden earth. Buddy estimated the number of stumps at thirty.

Several days later, at night, lying in his tent on his meager horse-hair mattress, under his two thin and short French army wool blankets, he thought of those stumps, after he had silently said his prayers.

They must have been a farmer's wood lot, he reasoned, as at Cherry Hill. A preserved storage of an essential—wood. Oak, poplar, or even cherry.

What of any downed logs that survived the artillery? Were they now shaped to shore up a trench, or floor a lorry, or create a box for ammunition— the sad ligaments of war?

Or, if splintered or shattered, were these remnants dissolving in the earth into their constituent chemicals, to succor any potential successors?

But once those trees had been massive, and alive. They had once yielded the vertical, bowed in chorus to, and bent by, the prevailing wind; they had budded into bright spring florets; their later leaves had danced in rhythmical response to the tempo of summer raindrops; those leaves had answered the fall call for color—cerise and amber—falling in flutters; the trees had survived the stark gelid winters. To begin anew.

Buddy drifted in sleep, remembering the tree that named the farm, at home.

....

On one such excursion, Sergeant Penzler pulled him aside and pointed out a small stand of trees, some newly splintered, some intact, about fifty yards away:

That's where the Germans would set up a machine gun emplacement—to fire on our flanks. Let's go look.

After entering the woods, Buddy saw a German soldier, his head resting on a tree trunk. His body was sprawled out down from the log. A loop of bowel hung by his side, covered with mud and flies, with maggots simmering upon it. A gnarled, clutching hand, already slipping skin, lay by his other side. His teeth glittered in his smoke-blackened face, like a vein of quartz in granite.

The German said:

Vater, vater!

Somehow, he was still alive. Sergeant Penzler said:

Water, he wants water.

Buddy reached for his spare canteen and started untwisting the cap.

Stop. Don't give him any water. He's gut shot. Water is precious up here, and he will die anyway. Go ahead and shoot the bastard now. We're not some damn charity.

Buddy could not believe what the sergeant said:

No!

The sergeant drew his .45 pistol and shot the German in his face. The back of his head exploded, sending fragments of bone and brain into the air and into the mud.

What are you, some kind of do-gooding son of a bitch? Get his belt buckle.

What?

Get his belt buckle!

No.

The sergeant drew his K-bar and cut the buckle off the German's belt. He showed it to Buddy. Inscribed on it: "GOTT MIT UNS." And put it in his backpack.

"God with Us," it says. God did not help that Hun bastard. All the Goddamn Germans wear one on their belts. That buckle is worth a couple of dollars American to those rear-echelon assholes. It's intact, worth saving. Maybe I'll get some decent hootch for it. Don't save the busted or broken ones.

Charity.

On the return to camp were heard distant scattered machine gun fire and harassing single artillery shells heading overhead towards the Germans. Penzler always instinctively ducked at their sound.

....

At the start of the offensive, on September 26, 1918, the American units on the first line, from left to right in the valley, were these divisions:

77th (New York National Guard)
28th (Pennsylvania National Guard)
35th (Kansas and Missouri National Guard)
91st (Regular Army)
37th (National Guard units from several small states)
79th (Regular Army)
4th (Regular Army)
80th (Kentucky and West Virginia National Guard)
33rd (Illinois National Guard):

The 33rd Division was in reserve. Though appearing to be masses of men, actually each portion of the front to which they were assigned was narrow, slightly more than two miles, and thus of great depth. Behind the infantrymen were many more soldiers of the same division supporting—artillery, communications, supply, medical, engineer, trucks, horses, carts, headquarters. Only about 15% of the division would actually fight.

....

Our lead arrived in Cambrai and was stored in the yard, the bars cross-stacked in orderly rows. In 1914, the Germans overran French and English defenses, and occupied Cambrai. They would stay there for four years.

In 1915, German acquisition officers noticed the lead bars and requisitioned them. All was shipped to Franz Heller and Son, German scrap metal dealers in Düsseldorf. These officers, being German, made detailed records: the length, width, and weight of each lead bar, the number of bars, when acquired, from whom, a receipt from the shipping firm, and a line, left blank. That was the line for the amount paid.

....

The goal of the first day's attack was Montfaucon. Even though the German first line of defense was mainly a lightly defended observation line, it took two days to be penetrated and overwhelmed. The attack then stalled and Montfaucon was still miles away, and the second line of defense remained only dented, still intact. The battle ended, for two days—the Americans exhausted, their supplies, their artillery bogged down on the ruined roads behind.

Why? Because there were only three original French roads north, none paved and repeatedly torn up by both armies artillery. The engineers tried to quickly repair them, and build other new ones. They failed miserably and all turned to mud. Logistics were terrible. Little food, water, or ammunition reached the front. And the wounded could not be transported to the rear for medical aid. The artillery could not advance to support the troops. It was chaos.

....

At 2 p.m. on September 30, orders were received for the 32nd Division to replace the 37th on the front line the next day. That division had been decimated attacking the second German defensive line, two miles short of its anchor, Mont Falcon. The entire attack, across the twenty-mile front, by all the divisions, had faltered, badly.

In echelon, the regiments of the 32nd division were sent forward through the night, the 127th and the 129th in the van, with attendant confusion, some platoons from each intermingled with the other.

On the way forward, they passed old collapsed German trenches, remnants of the original German line of defense. Buddy glanced to his left and saw at the bottom of a trench a hand, fully exposed to the wrist. It was turned upward with fingers clenched. It looked like a claw. Buddy closed his eyes, turning away. But the vision was etched on his retinas. The hand had been mottled, tinted between gray and green. But not decayed, perhaps preserved by chemicals in the soil. Buddy paused, shuddered, and removed his left hand from his rifle. He opened and closed it, repeatedly, studying the marvelous motion. But the anguish and agony of despair deeply concentrated in his consciousness.

On October 3, Company F was installed in the abandoned trenches of the 37th, in a line stretching for 200 yards, westward of the substantial village of Gesnes, mainly destroyed, facing a portion of what was called the Chen Sec woods. Mount Faucon was three miles to the east.

The German line crested on a small rising, designated as Hill 269 on the Army map, based up its height. Before their trenches was an open field, 250 yards from the German line. The next day was spent shoring up the trenches. They used pieces of timber salvaged from wrecked houses in Gesnes, some still sweating where split by their axes. Sporadic explosions were heard to the rear throughout the day, German artillery probing, turning soil into tilth. They were told to inspect their weapons, add extra ammunition, and be prepared for immediate action, though no time was given. That night was quiet—no sounds of war. A moon, early in its orderly procession, measuring neither days or years, was meekly shining in the night sky. Scant scouting snowflakes tasting the air.

. . . .

At 5 a.m. on October 7, 1918, the platoons of Company F, 127th, were quietly awakened by sergeants, addressed by their lieutenants, and told they were to attack at 6:00 a.m. The 3rd platoon was to lead Company F.

Don't worry. Our artillery has taken theirs out, someone said.

It had not. Buddy knew, from talking to older soldiers, that "our artillery" was manned and serviced by Americans, but there was no American artillery. It was French made and called a French 75 for its caliber—and made in the thousands, sometimes shoddily, with defective barrels. And those barrels caused projectiles to be off-line, or short, hitting Allied troops. Veterans said the French tested the 75s and those imperfect were given to the Americans.

And thus, during the night before several short rounds exploded just thirty-five yards beyond the American trenches —showering loosened dirt upon the soldiers with the concussions. Men wiped dust from their faces, clawed this shattered debris from around their collars and cleaned it off the bolts of their 1903 Springfields. Buddy inspected his rifle, again and again, and tried the locking mechanism for his bayonet.

The next morning, Lieutenant McCullough advised: "Just run across the field and attack. But spread out, and fix bayonets. Do not stop for a wounded man. Keep moving. They will be cared for. Secure the tree line. Take no prisoners, finish them off."

Buddy remembered the opening lines from the novel *Fortitude*: "It's not life that matters, but the courage you bring to it."

But a blending of terror and resignation engulfed Buddy. No time to think before acting. For all those attacking, there was no past, only the only lonely terrorizing now.

An iron morning sky, its dull light screening the sun. A flight of birds, free, etching themselves across the sky. The field, slightly misted, covered with cut corn stalks, edged with sward, gently rising toward the woods ahead. In those woods there appeared, dimly, to be a sort of concrete structure, some kind of bunker, about 300 yards ahead, partially hidden behind the tree line. The tree line began at the base of a hill, designated Hill 289 by its height. A light rain began. Buddy's shadow became pale.

Lieutenant McCullough screamed, forgetting to blow his whistle to order the charge:

Go!

The 3rd platoon was to lead, as ordered, with the rest of company F, the second and 3rd platoons following, The 3rd started, yelling and half running, weighed down by their packs and weapons. Immediately the ground seemed to explode under them. The saplings in the woods ahead, near the structure, waved back and forth, like a pendulum clock, then splintered from the blast of the German artillery behind.

Glowing lead motor shells arched over, like deadly meteors. Holes developed in the field where the shells landed, into which men tried to seek protection, scraping at the dirt with their hands, trying to get deeper, pleading for aid from the gravity of the core of the world. Radiant metal showers, as lava from an eruption, poured down, as from some celestial cauldron, smothering the field. Explosions, deafening, arrived every five or ten seconds, almost continuous. Clods of earth, roots of plants, iron fragments, parts of bodies were flung into the air.

The whining of shrapnel. Black smoke and the smell of cordite. The terror of being buried alive. Never found. Never home. No breath. No air. Missing in Action.

Bullets were kicking up dirt, in irregular stitches, pinging off stones in the ground. The flashes of the machine guns in the woods looked to Buddy like the flashing of fireflies—lightning bugs—seen on summer nights at home, in hundreds once marvelously flashing together in unison on a bush.

Men were screaming, crying out to God, for their mothers. Some dying with a stuttering, unconscious motion, a final unwinding. Some calling out—'medic, medic, medic'— pausing, repeated in threes, a tribal plea of fear and pain, volume steadily diminishing. Most crossed the thin final border between ecstasy and death. The rain strengthened. Each drop pocked the water in the shell craters, as painting the surface of beaten tin.

Buddy looked to his left where a shell had just exploded, and in the dirt arising he saw a body, a half of one body, lifted into the air. The lower half, split diagonally, with feet upended, rising, and then reversing, with coils of red and purple, coralline, intestines, hanging down, falling into the shell hole. He paused, disbelieving what he had seen and, retching, continued forward. Drops of blood had fallen upon his uniform, but he did not see them. The shells made an increasing sound as they arrived—like a terrible whistle on a train approaching. Buddy's hearing fell to a constant roar in his ears. But a taste of blood, copperish, accenting the swilling air, alighted on his tongue.

He stopped and lay down. Prone position. Within a minute, he saw a German soldier running forward from the tree line. Buddy was a good shot with his 1903 Springfield. Had he not been labeled a sharpshooter back at Camp Lee? He chambered a round and fired. The bullet hit the German in the chest and the soldier turned slightly to the right, tumbled forward, never losing his helmet, but remained un-moving on the tattered ground. Buddy quickly worked the bolt on his rifle, chambering another .303 round. He shot another German running parallel to the tree line, probably trying to get alway. He hit him, apparently in the right leg, and he too fell down. He was pushing with both arms, trying to arise when Buddy worked the bolt again, fired and the German's head exploded, with a red mist arising. Buddy could not believe what he had done. It had happened too fast. But when one sighted down the barrel of a rifle, his vision, in a circle of decreasing circumference, reduced until he saw nothing but the target. They were not squirrels, not rabbits. He began crying, tears marking a trail down through his dust covered cheeks. He vomited. Why had he been so fine shooting his old .22 rifle?

He stood, looking about for nonexistent cover. With no notice, a blow hit his left arm, well above his elbow—as if hit with great force by an iron rod— spinning him around and hurling him backward. His helmet spun backwards, likewise, his chin strap having been sliced by a piece of shrapnel that also sliced through the side of his cheek, from just below his ear to the side of his chin. Immense pain. He started to fall into a shell crater behind him. In that fall, he saw in the crater a white rock.

He thought:

Dr. Wills—quartz, silicon one, oxygen two. His head hit the rock and he was unconscious.

He had been in battle for nine minutes.

And the battle for the blasted heath which had been a cornfield ceased in forty minutes, for wont of combatants.

There was now no German artillery fire. An isolated and lonely rifle shot, its origin indeterminable. Wisps of smoke arising from shell craters, peacefully flowing to the west.

The remnants of the 3rd platoon, and the following 1st, had retreated to the trenches. The 2nd had never joined the battle. They were bunched up behind the forward ones.

Lieutenant Steiger and six members of the 3rd platoon had been killed. Sargeant Penzler survived.

In four days—October 4 to October 7— the 127th Regiment had suffered 131 soldiers killed in action, seventy who died of wounds, and 596 wounded.

....

The day after the battle in the cornfield, the 2nd platoon was sent to find any wounded. They were told to leave the dead. They would be taken care of later, sometime. Some dead were already cadaverine, becoming human brine, decay encouraged by chemicals in the shells which had killed them.

The soldiers entered the field, gingerly, wearily, carrying the makeshift stretchers they had learned how to construct. They noticed Buddy about twenty-five minutes into their search. He was still in his crater, still unconscious. Having determined he was still alive, they proceeded to remove him. Climbing down, one soldier took his legs, the other his arms. His face and neck, on the left side, were thick with dried blood. The one raising his left arm found it was totally limp, seemingly without substance. He was pulled up by his right arm and belt, and placed on the improvised stretcher. They folded the left arm across his chest. They did a quick check, looking for other wounds, but found none. They returned to the trench lines and continued on past them.

About 300 yards in their journey, the rear stretcher holder stumbled when he stepped into a mud hole. Buddy tumbled out, hit the ground, and cried out. It was the first sound he had made since he had been retrieved. They plunged a vial of morphine in his right leg. He remained unconscious, aided, perhaps, by the drug.

After another 200 yards they came upon a collection of carts, assembled with different soldiers, strangers, to transport the wounded to a temporary field hospital. After a conference between both sets of soldiers, Buddy, unconscious, was placed in a cart beside another soldier, who screamed out every time the cart bumped over rough ground. One of the new soldiers placed a red diagnosis tag on Buddy's shirt. It read: "Facial wounds; left arm injured."

The field medical unit was located in a small tent, manned by six medics and a single doctor. Beneath the collected carts dripped red droplets of blood, trickling down through their floors, with ants in columns, the columns straight and orderly, advancing towards their food.

The doctor picked up his left arm and rotated it, almost a complete circle. He knew there was terrible damage. The medics cleaned his face, rough stitched the wound, taped his left arm to his chest, confirmed the red diagnosis tag in their hurried examination, replaced his bloody tunic with a grey blouse, and injected a second vial of morphine. At the doctor's direction, they pinned a second tag, colored blue, on the blouse, one which authorized transportation to a permanent hospital, back in the encampment. Two lorries were parked behind the tent. Buddy was loaded into one, which awaited further wounded. Those wounded arrived, over a period of two hours: two unconscious as was Buddy, on similar stretchers; three sitting against the side boards; and three standing, holding on to the same. The lorry started toward the rear.

. . . .

Two hours later, the lorry arrived at the regimental hospital. It consisted of multiple large tents, each designated for particular use—though most were for delaying or convalescent needs, sized as to the degree of anticipated use. The balance were denominated for surgery. One, however, served as a temporary mortuary.

These tents had been erected on the grounds of a large chateau, one with minor damage repaired. It was surrounded by a hastily erected and flimsy fence.

The medical personnel—doctors, pharmacists, and nurses—were housed and fed in the chateau. Orderlies lived in a separate tent, with a handful of Army Regulars as perimeter guards. Medical supplies kept in outbuildings. Orderlies were used to transport the soldiers to the appropriate tent, consistent with their then medical needs, to deliver messages from medical personnel from one to another, to obtain and deliver requested medical supplies.

Before the chateau was a large cut-stone paved courtyard. It was here the lorries stopped, unloaded and placed stretcher cases, in orderly rows. Here Buddy's stretcher was laid.

And it was here that triage was performed—to assign degrees of urgency to the wounded soldiers and decide the order of treatment—by doctors—to decide who had a chance to live and who did not. That decision often need not be made. While awaiting the triage reconnaissance, soldiers died, their chests expanded and stilled, as if they had inhaled death.

This duty was voluntary. But it was logical, orderly, and necessary. It was usually performed by old doctors. Young doctors were found to be too compassionate, too sure of the skill of the medical arts, reluctant to make the final sad decision. Too often, their decisions wasted time and supply. It was the older doctors who performed this duty and made these decisions. The task was thankfully limited to about one half hour.

A doctor ascertained if a man was untreatable, certain to die. For those who seemed able to hear, or to understand, they offered assuring words of recovery. All, though, were quietly and gently given a lethal injection of morphine, a tiny, hollow misericordia. Then, pinned upon their clothing was a sullen silent yellow tag, a signal for Graves Registration personnel to act. The insignia on the uniform of Graves Registration was a colophon of death itself.

These judgmental doctors, always shaken, grey with sorrow and watered by tears, returned to a single small tent of one purpose. There they could choose two shots of the alcohol of their choice—Scotch, gin, bourbon, Irish, and grain—proffered and monitored by a silent sergeant. Most accepted this tiny consolation, before returning to the tent designated for their speciality of labor.

An investigating doctor, briefly feeling Buddy's left arm, re-taped it to his side, injected a limited dose of morphine, and determined he was to go to intermediate surgery—not urgent —and directed the stretcher bearers to transport him there.

10

The German scrap dealer planned to hold onto the lead. He knew the price of lead would rise as the war continued, and projected substantial profit. But the lead had cost them nothing, and they received nothing for it, for the German Army requisitioned it all on December 8, 1917. There was no government money available to pay for it at that time. Besides, the Fatherland needed the lead, desperately.

The lead bars were shipped by rail to Waffenfabrilik-Mauser, which owned three factories in Oberdorf am Necker, Wurttenberg. Two made rifles, the standard German infantry rifle—the Mauser 98. The third, bullets for that rifle. The required receipt for the shipment was never made, or lost. Our lead became a part of a 7.92 X 57 millimeter bullet, for the Mauser 98.

....

Buddy was placed in a hospital bed, unconscious from the recently injected morphine. The field dressing was removed from his facial wound. The cut was wide, having been hurriedly and poorly joined by only three stitches. A doctor removed those stitches, poured iodine over the wound, and attempted, with little success, to further close the wound. He re-stitched it closed with thirty-five stitches. It remained wide, two inches wide, a piercing stripe. It would turn purple, then red.

When Buddy awoke, in moderate pain, he was amazed to find himself washed, in a white hospital gown, on clean sheets, under a warm wool blanket. Beside his bed sat a middle aged nurse, in a long grey dress, with an ivory nurse's cap, a Red Cross adorning her head. She said her name was Edna. Buddy never knew the name of any other nurses.

She inquired:

Are you awake? Do you know where you are?

Buddy nodded yes.

She silently offered him a drink of water from a tall glass and he gulped it down. He had never been so thirsty in his life. He held the glass out twice and it twice was filled and devoured.

He said:

Thank you, ma'am. God bless you.

He lay back on his pillow. It was raining and windy, and he heard the undulating wet canvas. He fell asleep, not deeply, but only tiny tempests of sleep, a muffled restlessness.

The other wounded in this tent sometimes cried out, beacons of pain, terror, despair. Injections were given to quiet them. Too often, the sad, defeated countenance of their eyes was that of a dying animal. Sometimes, those eyes were closed, their faces covered, screening partitions erected, and a yellow tag attached to the end of a bed. Orderlies then summoned Graves Registration.

....

Still in the intermediate surgery tent, Buddy was visited by two doctors, a Dr. McManus, a general practitioner, and a Dr. Engh, a surgeon, at 7 a.m. They checked his serial number against his chart. They told him they were going to take a look at his arm. At their direction, a nurse had inserted herself between Buddy's side and his left arm, ostensibly to aid in removing the bandages and tape, but in truth to shield his eyes from what they believed they would see. They told him he would be given a local anesthetic to smother any pain, and the nurse injected one in Buddy's shoulder.

The arm was black, slack, with reddish streaks, the flesh

dissolving into deliquescence, all bone cassious. Both doctors massaged it. It felt like they were squeezing a cloth bag half filled with coffee beans. Lifting it by Buddy's hand, the upper arm simply dropped down, foundering on itself, supported solely by the thin tension of remaining skin. They directed the nurse to re-bandage it. She, still concealing the arm, re-bandaged and re-taped it to his side.

They walked about fifteen yards away. In hushed conversation, they conferred. Dr. McManus:

The humerus is pulverized, splintered, will never mend, and there is gangrene. The tibia and radius in the lower arm are intact, but they will become useless, of course. The scapula seems solid, so the socket can remain, perhaps a base for a prosthesis. Is there any choice but to amputate?

Dr. Engh replied:

No, it must be amputated, and soon.

As Dr. McManus left, Dr. Engh approached Buddy and advised him:

Well, son, there is some gangrene. It's caused by broken blood vessels, and they carry bacteria, germs. These germs can kill you. I am going to operate—probably the end of this week, or early next week—to remove that gangrene. Understand?

Buddy nodded yes.

But Dr. Engh, purposely, had cloaked his intention to amputate. Too often, in the past, such an announcement caused an eruption—cries of "NO, NO, NEVER; I WON'T PERMIT IT!"—tears, pleas, medically fantastic solutions.

As Dr. Engh and the nurse were leaving, he advised her, as he had already ordered in Buddy's chart:

I am going to operate early tomorrow morning, at five a.m. Please prepare him tonight, as usual, and so direct any subsequent nurse; but of course do not tell him what is to happen, or when. Silence like that smothers fears. It is best.

Following this oblique instruction, a nurse that evening approached Buddy. He was reading *Robinson Crusoe*, of which he had never heard before. He found it fascinating. During the day, a volunteer from the Red Cross had passed through the ward, offering books from a basket. Those who could not read, rather than admitting that state, usually raised their hand—stop—and with a smile, waved the volunteer on. Buddy has chosen, perhaps by random, this novel.

Soldier, the night nurses say you moan, sometimes cry out, in your sleep. It disturbs other patients. I have some medicine here which will offer you more sound sleep.

She proffered a large glass of water, which Buddy, distracted from his reading, obediently drank. After thanking the nurse, he returned to reading.

The water contained three tinctures, three concentrated extracts, of opium.

....

The next morning, Buddy was awakened at 4:30. He was groggy, fuzzy, bewildered from the opium. He was rushed into an operating room on a stretcher. There, his legs and his right arm were pinioned by leather straps to the white painted steel operating table. Feebly protesting, unsure what was happening, he was trying to rise, when his shoulders were pushed down, and a mask placed on his face, with a combination of chloroform and ether dripping down. He gasped twice, and was rendered unconscious.

....

Before operating, Dr. Engh always recited the distinctly remembered and succinctly stated instruction, in an essay by the Swiss Dr. Francisco Gonzales-Crussi: "...the movements of the scalpel admit of no hesitation and as always without return." The removal of the arm took ten minutes. Two flaps of skin, purposely left, were to be closed, tightly sewn to overlap, to cover a thoroughly cleaned socket of the scapula. Operating room nurses bathed the scapula socket and stump in water and alcohol, added a varnish of iodine, joined and sewed the two skin flaps to cover the exposed socket, and thickly bandaged and taped that terminal. Dr. Engh jotted down a terse note for inclusion in Buddy's chart, silently viewed the nurses' work, and without further words, departed.

Buddy was still unconscious as orderlies carried him to a

different bed, in a convalescent tent.

....

Buddy stumbled into semi-consciousness three hours later, following the operation. His eyes still shut, he reached out with his right hand. A monitoring nurse grasped it, and Buddy recognized it as that of another person. He thought, "I am still alive, still alive!" and fell again, reassured, into a deep sleep.

....

When Buddy was fully awake and cognizant, he immediately reached to feel his gangrene-free left arm. He felt no arm, and, half rising, acting as if he had lost an item to be quickly found, he grappled under his left side, then within his bedding.

He realized what had happened and began screaming:

NO, NO, NO!

An attending nurse pushed him back down upon the bed. She took his right hand, and said:

Calm down. It had to be done. You must understand this. The bones in your upper arm were crushed, splintered. They could never heal, never mend. It was useless, and also your lower arm. There was no way to attach that part. And the gangrene would kill you. You must understand. Your arm was useless, it could never be used. You have to accept this. There was no other choice.

Staring at the nurse, her words sinking into his mind, he turned his head to the right, pulled the blanket over it, and quietly sobbed.

....

For three days following the amputation, Buddy did not speak. Then, he came to realize, with bitter resignation, that what the nurse had said was true, there had been no choice. Yes, unpurged gangrene would have killed him. His arm had become useless. At least he was still alive.

With that understanding, Buddy began reading again. He had picked up *Robinson Crusoe*. In mid-sentence, a flood of imperative enquiries penetrated his mind. He lay back on his bed in the convelesent tent.

Why had God taken his arm? Why was he still alive, and

others in the 3rd platoon dead? Why were both Germans and Americans alike killed? How did God choose these conclusions? How can God make the dead alive again? And put back together, whole and healthy, those shattered, mangled parts of bodies? And, finally, did God answer, or even hear, his nightly prayers, his supplication for forgiveness, his proffered praise, his pleas for guidance in his forthcoming life?

No. That portion of the foundation of his life— that God directed, controlled, foreordained the life of mankind, and the physical universe—dissolved, evaporated in an instant. But he did not feel crushed or defeated by this perception, this creation of a void. He knew, now, his vanished belief had not been true; it was not in accordance with that which was real. It was not in accord with Nature. The dead do not arise. It had been a delusion, a fantasy, almost insanity. He did not know how he would fill this void; but he felt certain, somehow, he would, and then see things as they are.

He fell into a dreamless sleep.

....

In the convalescent tent, Buddy had a dream. On a cobalt blue background is an enormous radiant silvery circle of steel. At a pinion in its center is set a single rod, of the same material. That rod is like a single second hand on a clock. It sweeps out the circumference of the circle. Each sweep captures a minute. He is watching it from above.

He understands what it means: it is measuring the passage of time—time from all the eternity in the past to all the eternity in the future. He feels pain beginning, slowly but steadily, in orderly increments, increasing in intensity, as the sweeping continued. The pain reaches a peak of agony. But it will lessen and end, he knows, as time descends into the past, His eyes are fixated on the vision before him. But the single rod has stopped, it is catching, twitching, rapidly back and forward, back and forward, as if its mainspring had failed. And he realizes his pinnacle of pain will thus last forever. Time has stopped.

He abruptly awoke, screaming, terrified, until he, two

minutes later, understood, it was just a dream. Though still shaking, he soon fell into untroubled sleep.

....

Several days later, Buddy left the convalescent tent, as was permitted, if you promised to return within three hours. He wandered through the encampment, stepping around mud puddles, and came upon a temporary sign, affixed to the front of a tent. It was twilight. He was wearing his hospital garb, under his Army greatcoat, and his battered boots.
TODAY AT 4 P.M. REVEREND FLOURNOY TARWATER, D.D. WILL GIVE A SERMON FOR ANY PROTESTANT SOLDIER. THEY WILL BE MOST WELCOME TO HEAR HIS INSPIRING WORDS. PLEASE JOIN WITH HIM.

Though services had started—a hymn was ending—Buddy decided to enter. Tarwater had paused in the middle of a sermon. Buddy sat down in the rearmost row of individual folding chairs. That row was almost empty—only one person, a soldier in uniform, occupying. About fifty soldiers sat, scattered, in rows ahead.

Tarwater was tall, crowned by long white hair—a pretend Moses as pictured in the Bible—wearing a black cassock and a long black cape. His mouth was somehow lopsided, as if the muscles on the left side of his face had atrophied, with long incisors like fangs. His voice was shrill, not stentorian, and two registers too high.

He rose from a chair, constructed so as to be higher than usual, and painted gold.

Now, my dear friends, I shall continue my remarks. They shall begin with quotations from the Old Testament. Words that describe your sacred cause, your sacred duty, here in France in this war. First, Joshua 10:19: And stay you not, but pursue after your enemies, and attack their rear guard. Do not allow them to enter their cities, for the Lord your God hath delivered them into your hand. Remember, it was he who tumbled down the walls of an evil city, Jericho. The encamped Germans are evil. The German filth is just north of this once fair city. Their city is where they are now. They have been, by their hideous actions, delivered to your hands, and your vengeance. It

*is God's will. And from Judges 21:11: And this is the thing ye shall
do. You shall utterly destroy every male.*

Tarwater continued:

*Fear not death in battle. Remember God is with us, He is with
each of you. And God shall deliver the just victory to you, by you.
Let me pause while you place deeply in your memory what God had
decreed, speaking through me. Let me pause here, to regain my
breath.*

And he sat down on his golden chair.

Buddy erupted, screaming, trembling with rage, quickly
walking down the center aisle, his greatcoat flaring, shaking
and pointing with his one arm, his fingers clamped.

He shouted:

*You lying bastard, you fool! Don't you understand anything? You
say, "God is with us." Every German has those words stamped on
his belt buckle. Who is God with—us or them? Does God want more
acres and acres of death, miles and miles of death, over the oceans,
throughout the whole Earth—Americans and Germans—and all men
—not just them or us? Does God really determine the affairs of man?
Does God care what happens to us? You are not a righteous man; you
are not just a fool. You are evil, corrupt, a messenger of death.*

Buddy continued toward the raised floor on which the altar
and golden chair stood. Tarwater stood, retreating behind his
golden chair, fearing that Buddy would strike him.

Stop him, stop him!, he shrieked.

Two soldiers in the first row stood and reached for Buddy.
One grabbed his right arm, and the other, searching for the left,
surprised at an empty sleeve, grabbed the rear of Buddy's
pants. Buddy was crying as they dragged him down the aisle,
to the rear of the tent. All present had stood, watching in
amazement. The soldiers threw Buddy outside. He landed face
down in a mud puddle.

Reverend Tarwater terminated his remarks. There was no
benediction. He had no further words. Dragging his golden
chair, he departed, silently, behind the curtain. His arrogant,
self-presumed righteous superiority had destroyed any moral
restraint.

The soldiers exited the tent, silently, slowly, gingerly stepping aside Buddy, each pausing to look at him, and continued upon their various ways.

Twilight had become night.

Twenty minutes later, Buddy, pulling himself forward out of the puddle with his right arm, kneeled while his mind cleared, and then stood.

He walked on and came across a wooden building, of use not named, about thirty feet square without a continuous foundation—rather, its four corners supported by pillars of bricks, as was Cherry hill, though there were massive rocks of white quartz serving that function.This floor was raised two and one half feet, more widened than had been his bunk on the *Charybdis*. He crawled under. It was dry, and, using his greatcoat as a blanket and his right arm as a pillow, fell asleep, hearing within the ticks of silence. He was awakened, at 4 a.m., by a print of the slanting early sun bathing his face. He found in his mind a thought fixed and firm: that he be prepared for the future, a future he could not discern but one he felt would require supplies.

11

Still filthy, even more bedraggled, Buddy walked west through the camp until he saw a loosely constructed wooden building displaying a sign which read: "Supply, 127 Regiment." It was 6:30 in the morning. The thought had remained steadfastly in his mind: He needed to be prepared. He paused and entered the building.

There was no one in the building except a bulky figure sitting behind an enormous battered wooden desk, feet crossed at the ankles and resting on top of that desk. No boots, some carpet slippers.

He was an old Army master sergeant, displaying no name on his uniform. His face, not recently shaved, was creased like a dried apple, appeared sand blasted from ancient acne, with tiny deltas of wrinkles radiating from the corners of his eyes. Only fringes of white hair circled his head. He wore a heavy Army wool greatcoat. Buddy's greatcoat was muddied and torn, held together by mis-aligned buttons.

Boy, you are a mess. What happened? Did you sneak out of the hospital, find some good bourbon, get drunk and pass out in a mud puddle? Do you have any bourbon left? No? Damn. You need to get cleaned up. Are you in the 127th?

Buddy, slowly nodding, replied:

Company F

He then handed Buddy a sliver of soap, two small towels,

and a pair of Army underwear. His voice was deep southern, Alabama or Mississippi.

Out back there is a line of rain barrels, in front of the sandbags. The fool engineers built this thing on a slope, and it would flood. So, sandbags and rain barrels. Throw those dirty clothes, and those boots, on the pile of the ruined stuff out there. They're supposed to pick it up, but of course they never have. I reckon you're not going back to the hospital. Don't blame you. Those places are too sad. Now, while you're doing that I shall have a little nip. I need it to get going in the morning if I'm going to do my duty. See you when you get back

From a drawer in the battered desk, he removed an unlabeled quart green colored bottle and took a swig. He pulled out a small cigar, a cheroot, from his breast pocket and struck a French lucifer on a piece of rock holding down some papers on the desk, and lit up.

Buddy said: Yes, sergeant, and exited the tent.

Dipping water from a rain barrel with his hand, using one towel as a washcloth, he scrubbed as best he could and dried off with the other. As instructed, he threw his clothes and boots on the enormous pile and put on his fresh underwear.

He returned to the tent, embarrassed at his appearance. The sergeant appeared to be dozing and Buddy stood silently before the desk until the sergeant noticed him.

Well, boy, that's better. I see you gave an arm to the general. I've seen it time after time, over the years. A crime. The general makes a plan. He thinks it's brilliant. The duties are reduced downward, narrowed to the size of every unit. And the captains say to the majors: "My company can do it, sir!" Are the lesser officers going to tell the truth?: "This is crazy!" Hell, no. And up it goes—to the bird colonels and then to the general. All these officers, kissing ass, have expressed appreciation of the plan. What the hell else could they do? They want to be promoted. The general concludes his plan is indeed brilliant.

But the general is not going to get his head exploded or his balls shot off. He will be sitting on his fat ass, in a mansion he directed the engineers to fix up, drinking good whiskey and smoking good cigars, even Cuban. And when the plan falls apart, when the soldiers are

*dead or wounded or missing—it is not his fault. It's the fault of those
below him. He starts on a new plan. The general's plan for this sorry
place. So many soldiers are gone. I have three times enough gear and
rations, they brought a passel of rations yesterday, and medical
supplies, for what's left of the 127th. I hear it ain't much. And I hear
those remaining are desperate for ammunition, transportation,
artillery shells. Fuck the general. Take as much as you want of
anything here. I like the canned peaches best. Take your favorites. I
gave up keeping records. The general would never read them,
anyway.*

Buddy chose: two large backpacks, a duffle bag, two
blankets, one rubberized half-shelter, three pair of underwear,
three tunics, two trousers, a belt, Army green utility shirts,
pants and hat, a wool greatcoat, three pair of socks, a scarf, five
packs of waterproof matches, a K-Bar knife, an engineer's
hatchet, a tin cup a mess kit and two canteens. Also, twenty-
five days of rations. Finally, a new pair of boots, which he
carefully fitted. Setting all aside, he dressed with additional
gear. He put on as much the clothing as he could wear,
doubling layers.

From another section of the building, opening medical
supplies, he gathered bandages, adhesive tape, a tourniquet,
tubes of antiseptic cream, bottles of iodine and a bottle of
cleansing alcohol. All he gathered was brand new.

He stuffed all not being worn into the backpacks and duffle
bag, one on his back, the other and the duffel bags dragged
across the floor. He stopped before the sergeant, fearing he had
taken too much, and would be cursed, or worse.

But the sergeant said nothing about the gear. He said:

*Take one of those carts over there and put that stuff in it, covering
it with a blanket. If anyone asks you, tell them you're taking it to the
goddamn general. Wait, I will get a package of pins, to hold up that
left sleeve.*

Buddy did as directed, choosing a small cart, though large
enough to hold both backpacks, the duffel bag, the rations and
the medical supplies.

He returned to face the sergeant and said:

Thank you, sergeant, I shall never forget what you have done.

The sergeant replied, for the first time, with a small smile on his face:

Take care, son. I know you are a Southerner, probably from Virginia by your accent. There are few of us in the 127th. We must always look out for one another. It is best you leave now, while we are alone.

Tears welled in Buddy's eyes, and he turned his head, so the sergeant would not see them.

Walking out, dragging his cart, Buddy noticed three large boxes labeled YMCA, full of books. He chose the middle one, the books not stacked but tumbled together, and he probed through them. There were some novels he had never heard of, obscure histories, some poetry, and many Bibles of different publishers. He came upon an almost new complete Shakespeare. That alone he placed in his cart.

....

After loading his cart at the 127th supply tent, Buddy walked south, following an old earthen road, though one scored and deepened with old cart and wagon tracks, a shallow ochre furrow, for about four miles, into what clearly had in former times been farm country. On a slight rise to the right was a once substantial farmhouse, at the end of a curving path about thirty yards long. The farmhouse was now broken, no doubt hit by long range German artillery during the siege of Verdun years ago, and now abandoned.

Only its left wall, two-storied, was intact, the others crumbled. But hanging from the top of the left wall were solid floor or ceiling timbers, at a forty-five-degree angle, completing an isosceles triangle with the slate floor—a pergola offering refuge.

It was deep twilight when Buddy entered this war-created cave, and he was exhausted. He pulled his cart within, and using a corner of a duffel bag as a pillow and his greatcoat as a blanket, he immediately fell asleep. He would examine this structure in the morning.

....

An ingot of sunlight awoke him. At first he did not know where he was, but as his mind stabilized, he remembered his gathering from the old master sergeant, and his discovery of this partial farmhouse building. Rousing himself, he drank from one of the canteens, and ate a ration of hard biscuit.

He began exploring, wondering if any items of use remained, purposely discarded, or left, when those who had lived here departed. The cave-like structure was about ten feet wide, declining, slanting, from its highest point of fifteen feet, to the slate paved floor, and about twenty-five feet deep, ending in a pile of stone rubble.

He found a large quarter-crushed wooden box, dove-tailed corners, with a top intact. Inside, he found two thick heavy green long curtains, and a damask pillow printed with day lilies, and a small soft leather bag with a drawstring. It smelled of tobacco—it would hold his remaining six silver dollars. He set them aside. Later, he found a debris-protected cardboard box, with three unbroken, and fifteen partial, candles. Of last discovered potential use, in an armoire turned, probably when falling, upside down, were articles of clothing, saved from rain by a mass of torn and ruined clothing, of indescribable character, atop them: a black men's suit; three shirts—white, white, blue—missing the detachable collars; a heavy wool gray sweater with a fat, round neck, as the Scots seaman had worn on the *Charybdis*.

The addition of these items to the cart would require him to thereafter carry a duffle bag, with a lengthened strap. It would be carried on his right shoulder, looped over his head, hanging to the left, protecting his stump.

Outside, fronting the farmhouse, was a similarly paved length of porch, facing northeast, as was the house; a view of the Meuse, miles away, and the Ardennes in the distance. There was a stone bench, worn down at its center, from generations it had accommodated. When Buddy first sat on this bench, he examined it and found it sandstone. Though its feet existed, a sizable chunk of one corner was broken off, no doubt during the shelling. Buddy added it to the accumulated pile of items. It could sharpen a K-Bar, or a hatchet. The curtains would be a mattress, candles for light, and the clothing?

....

On the afternoon following his first night in the abandoned farmhouse, Buddy sat on the sandstone bench and started thinking of the future.

What could he do at home? Or, rather, what could he not? His depression increased in proportion to an increasing list:

He could not split wood;

he could not keep a plough rigid, behind a horse or a mule, to carve a straight furrow; he could not accurately fire a rifle for game;

he could not bridle, or saddle, a horse;

he could not pluck and clean a Guinea hen for cooking; he could not carry any heavy object; and,

he could only carry one bucket of water, up from the spring.

The nurse had said his left arm was rendered useless. Was he? At home, he knew, age and despair would only expand his worthlessness—until he became a parasite at Cherry Hill, draining his family, and all his pride.

But in an insight, he thought:

I am not useless.

He remembered fellow soldiers saying that if they were killed, they had "bought the farm." The U.S. Government promise of $10,000 would benefit his mother, and whoever in his family inherited, to keep Cherry Hill viable for years, as their home.

And, further, there would never be an Ann Davis in his future, or any girl approximating her. What girl would want a useless man, and one with a vivid two-inch wide red scar, marking the entire left side of his face? There would be no future for her, either.

His thought mirrored that of Cicero:

I cannot forget things I wish to forget.

But then, he remembered Dr. Wills's recital of Epictetus:

You should not be concerned over that which you have no control;

you should only be concerned over that which you do control—the way to live your life.

He would forget Cherry Hill. He had to. Or he would go mad. Though his future at Cherry Hill, in Culpeper, in Virginia, had dissolved as a wisp of dying candle smoke, Buddy reached a resolution, and a compelling path to follow.

But when?

....

That night, Buddy bought a curtain out from the farmhouse and spread it on the ground beyond the paved entrance way. He added the damask pillow. He lay down and gazed upwards.

The sky was as clear as black glass. There was no moon, or clouds. The atmosphere was perfectly transparent. The stars are crescent, gleaming, sharpened in view.

Buddy noted their various colors—white, red, blue, green— the same as in some streaks in marble. Those colors must be caused by the same chemicals, there as here.

A blended torrent of Dr. Wills's words flooded his mind:

Everything in the universe is made of chemicals. All chemicals have existed for all time in the past, and will exist for all time in the future. And they bind together in different ways, but always in an orderly manner, according to the same unchanging laws, the same unchanging mathematics. Some of those chemicals forming the stars are part of me; and some of those chemicals forming me are part of the stars. I am part of the stars, and the stars are part of me. Just then, a meteor passed over his head, A point of light, with a golden corona, trailing fiery embers, arching to the east, falling beyond sight past the mountains. He recognized a falling star.

Whether the meteor be burnt or buried, as had been his left arm, as they decompose, their chemicals would become part of the earth, awaiting a new order of arrangement, perhaps as a spring, perhaps as a strand of a girl's hair.

All Dr. Wills had said was true, and had led to this rapture, this revelation. Buddy remembered St. Matthew had said:

Seek and ye shall find. (Mathew 7:7) No, he thought, you may seek, but you will not find. The truth must find you.

And Ariel's song from *The Tempest*: "Nothing of him that doth fade, But doth suffer a sea-change, into something rich and strange."

Nature is orderly. God is Nature.

Buddy had found a new foundation of faith for his life: I am a portion of the Universe, and the Universe is a portion of me.

....

The morning following his revelation, in the night on the hill at the abandoned farmhouse, Buddy walked back to the Army encampments outside Verdun. He entered a tent with a wooden sign posted outside: Graves Registration, 127th Regiment.

Inside were five privates, furiously typing at individual desks. On the opposite side of the tent were seven steel boxes with lids, on a long wooden table. Each had taped on the outside consecutive dates, beginning Oct 3 and ending Oct 10 and each with the letters KIA/DW (KILLED IN ACTION/ DIED OF WOUNDS).

One clerk looked up and said, pointing at the long table:

We haven't even got to those. We are way behind. What the hell is going on up there?

Buddy said nothing. Walking along the row, with his back to the clerks, he quietly opened a box and dropped his identification disk in. The box was labeled Oct 7. Nodding at the clerks, he walked out of the tent. He felt certain, and he was proved right, that his identity disk would never be correlated to the paper daily reports which were supposed to be supplied by each lieutenant—many dead lieutenants, too much paper lost or intelligible, too much chaos.

Later he remembered:

October 7, Dr. Wills's birthday.

He wondered if his choice of dates was truly random— somehow orderly.

Graves Registration periodically entered the tent, depositing identification discs, as their duty required, and collecting the contents of the boxes, every week.

....

The planners had conceived of the fantastic idea of building a road up into the Ardennes bordering the Meuse, its height lengthening the range of artillery to perpendicularly strike the entire German second line of defense, anchored on Mount Falcon, from East to West across the valley. They had never, of course, considered the effort might be better spent on improving the roads North from Verdun, so as to be closer to, and follow, the American battle line, as logic should have dictated.

Thus the engineers built a sturdy bridge across the Meuse, directly east of Verdun, and a road upwards, until it met a ridge extruding from the west face of the mountain, discovered by an advanced engineer team, a ridge steadily rising at about five degrees—natural roadway to the left. In geological terms, it was a "nappe."

But when this road was half-built, at a height of about 1,000 feet above the valley floor, and only 200 yards along the ridge, the German second line of defense had crumbled. Mont Falcon was in ruins, occupied. The Germans had begun a vicious stubborn defense between the second and third lines, and were strengthening the latter. All to gain time for their troops to complete an orderly withdrawal toward the Fatherland.

No American artillery had ever crossed the bridge.

....

Pulling his cart, Buddy crossed the abandoned new bridge over the Meuse. He followed the half-built road upward, and then turned onto the extruded ridge to the left, rising and curving to the north. Where the construction shortly thereon ended, a narrow trail continued, probably an old animal one, intermittently wide enough, and when necessarily broadened by use of his engineers hatchet, to accommodate the cart.

He followed this path; it was covered with soil, moss, clumps of grass and was overhung and underhung with scrubby pines. He had traveled about three miles, when an opening in pine growth abruptly appeared, bursting with sunlight, and the path shorn of cover. The arced path became paved, of a sort, with smooth rock, a rock Buddy recognized as granite. It was tilted downward at about four degrees over a breath of nine feet. This opening extended about forty yards—probably only 1/5000th of the circumference of the mountain —before continuing in the foliage and cover as before.

To the west, the entire twenty-mile-wide valley could be seen, the ruined Mount Falcon, and in a haze, the edge of the Argonne Forest. In military terms, it was a "coign of advantage."

The exposed mountain face on the right was chalk, a layer about 300 feet high, with a small crescent of sandstone visible at its peak. Directly below the peak, an opening in the chalk wall had become a cave.

This narrow section of the mountain faced northwest, and directly into the heart of prevailing wind, of the rainstorms and snowstorms crossing the valley. These weathering instruments had, over thousands of years, eroded the chalk surface inward, leaving the more dense and harder supporting granite layer more intact.

A weakness in the chalk engendered the formation of the cave. It was about twenty-five feet wide and nine feet tall at the top of the rounded arch which formed its entrance. Those dimensions remained intact for about twenty-five feet inward, then gently narrowing to end in the darkness. The floor of the cave was granite too. The tilt of this layer had swept out any detritus of chalk fallen within, carried by and with any accumulated water dripping from the porous roof of the cave over the edge of the ledge.

To the left of the entrance fell an unbroken stream of clear water, at eye level and above, three inches round, accumulated from the sandstone layer which lay above. Unbroken in part, the upper half of the stream tumbled and broke over rough places in the face of the chalk, but then struck a six-inch-long protuberance of chert, flint, formed within the chalk, directing it outwards enough to rejoin and steady.

I shall live here, for a while.

He reasoned that with his civilian clothes, and his six remaining silver dollars, he could walk back down to Verdun and buy food, or other necessities. He now knew what those dollars were worth—at least in Paris—perhaps even more in Verdun. He could sit there, listen, and maybe pick up enough French to be basically understood. Or discover a gracious Frenchman, who knew some English. He estimated the trip would take two and half hours, each way.

Buddy unloaded his cart. The mattress was the thick curtain, overlaying pine branches, which had yielded to the engineer's hatchet. A constructed canopy upheld the rubberized shelter half over the bed. Blankets and the greatcoat would cover him. Supplies, those least vulnerable to water stored on top, were placed in the side eves of the cave where water seldom fell. A small fire ring of discovered pieces of crumbled sandstone was formed on the granite, just outside the cave entrance. The cart, turned sideways, protected the entrance from wind and rain.

....

One morning, a German sniper, part of the left wing of the temporary defensive line before the the third German line, was perusing the mountain, looking upward, across the Meuse, with his telescopic sight. He was sitting looking out of a second-story window in an abandoned farmhouse. A flash of light caught his eye, and he returned the scope to examine it.

It was a man, dressed in what he recognized as U.S. Army green utilities, sitting on a ledge of rock. Behind him rose a narrow wall of whitish mountain face, though the man was silhouetted before something oval and darker. He concluded the man was a U.S. Army spotter, spying on German defenses, probably ranging and targeting for American artillery.

He adjusted his scope to make the scene more definite. He gauged distance, droppage, and windage, and corrected the sights on his Mauser 98(s), as dictated by these parameters. After this correction, and raising the rifle again, he saw the man was standing up. The target was green, surrounded by white on a dark background. It was an ideal set-up.

He reached in a bag at his side and selected a single bullet, a Mauser 7.92 x 57 mm, from a stripper clip, as snipers do, lowered his rifle and inserted it. He raised his rifle and sighted again. The man had not moved. Holding his breath, he gently squeezed the trigger, as he had been taught. The bullet left the muzzle of his Mauser 98(s) at a velocity of 2,096 feet per second.

The lead in that bullet contained our lead.

....

Buddy was standing just in front of the cave entrance. He was watching, entranced, a single eagle, its wings only occasionally flapping, soaring over the valley. Its feet were raised against its body, their ends downward, joined together, as if in prayer. Perhaps, he thought, a prayer to Nature.

The sniper's bullet hit Buddy at an upward angle, slightly to the left of his breastbone, exploded his heart, and exited his back, then falling, its power expended. But its former velocity thrust Buddy backward and down on his back inside the cave. He experienced no pain. He died in thirty seconds. The final countenance of his eyes were quizzical, then resolute.

....

Chalk is less dense, less rigid, more porous than the limestone or the marble into which it may, through the heat and pressure of metamorphasis, evolve. Buddy's body was never found.

Three years after his death, the chalk cave collapsed and sealed itself, chalk filling the entire former void. His body dissolved into its constituent chemicals—perhaps one day, commingled with others in orderly arrangement, to become a streak in a portion of marble, with an adjacent nugget of lead.

Author's Notes

This is a work of fiction. That said, the work is one nonetheless structured on facts. Those facts include the following:

The Green Family existed. Ann Eliza Green was the author's grandmother. James Lewis, known as Buddy, was the author's great uncle. They were raised on Cherry Hill farm. That farm and the town of Culpeper, the hamlet of Amissville, and the Amissville Methodist Church now exist, though described as in earlier times

The Green family retained many memories of Buddy's life. Each of the items below is original, as is the portrait on the book cover. The postcard pictured in the body of the work is the actual one received, after being re-addressed by a postmaster, by Buddy Green.

The Green family saved Buddy's letters home. The letterhead of each in the body of the work is correct, as is the place of origin. The tone of each letter is truthful, while some of the language has been created. But the tone throughout his letters is one reflecting his belief he would be killed. The phrase: "I have a horror of going across" was actually Buddy's language in one letter.

The author tried to obtain Buddy's individual military

record. He learned that those records, among thousands had been destroyed by fire at an Army warehouse in St. Louis, Missouri, many years ago. He was able to obtain, however, a copy of the actual page of the 127th Regiment, Company F weekly status report, showing Buddy (and one Corporal and five other privates) killed in action on October 7, 1918. That is the only individual mention of him in the military record.

Buddy Green was killed at a location quite near that described in the novel, as deduced from World War I histories of both the 127th Regiment and the 32nd Division. He is buried in the American Meuse-Argonne Military Cemetery in France, as pictured.

* * *

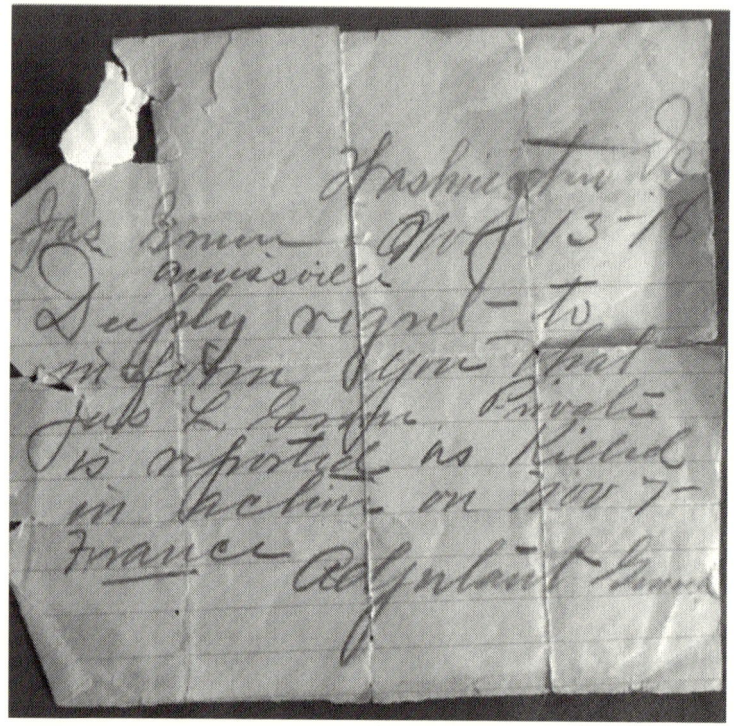

There was an error either in the creation or the
transcription of this telegram, dated November 13, 1918.
The telegram reads "November" rather than the correct
"October 7" for the date of death. A message notifying of
a death could not reach Washington from the Meuse-
Argonne in the six days between November 7 and
November 13. This is the original received by the family.

....

The American Military Cemetery, at Romagne-Sous-

Mont Falcon, France, was dedicated on May 30, 1937. It was beautifully designed and magnificently constructed. It remains intact.

There is a gravestone for each of those killed in the Meuse-Argonne Offensive of 1918. The graves are designated by Plot, Row, Grave. There are 14,246 graves.

* * *

This gravestone is in Plot D, Row 19, on Grave 27. It recites Buddy's actual unit, 127th Infantry Regiment, 32nd Division. It does not include his actual Company F.

* * *

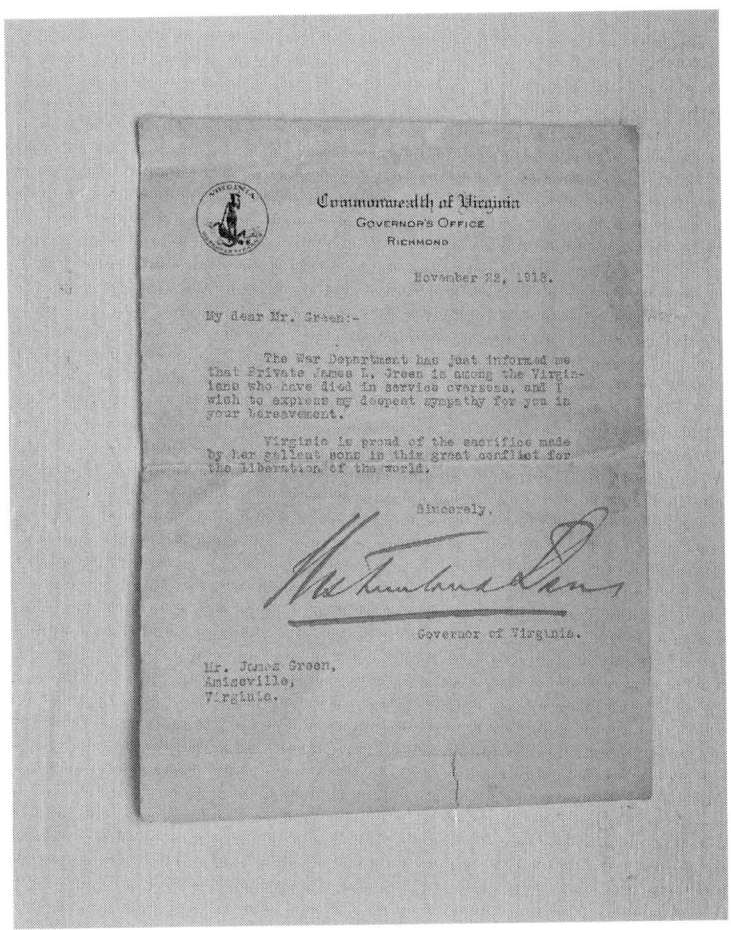

Buddy Green's father did not survive him. The above
was received by his family.

This was received by the Green family.

ABOUT THE AUTHOR

James W. Haley, Jr., and his wife of 55 years, Ann Davis Haley, live in Fredericksburg, Virginia. They have three children and seven grandchildren.

Haley is a Senior Judge of the Court of Appeals of Virginia. Haley now owns Cherry Hill, and the farm shall remain in his family, where one day his ashes shall be placed.

His paternal grandmother, Eliza Ann Green, married William Ashton Haley, of Front Royal, Virginia.

In summers as a young boy, Haley would spend weeks at Cherry Hill, aiding his maiden great aunt, Odessa Lee Green, who resided there alone. Among other chores, he split wood, carried water from the spring, and worked the garden. In those times, there was no electricity or a well.

Odessa's brother, James Lewis Green, was James Haley's great uncle.

As recited, Buddy Green was killed in action on October 7, 1918, and is buried in the Meuse-Argonne Cemetery. Judge and Mrs. Haley alone of his family have visited his grave, the source of the earlier photograph.

Made in the USA
Middletown, DE
05 February 2023

23530178R00080